MW00680870

WE HAVE NOT BEEN LISTENING

A NOVEL

THE AWAKENING

WE HAVE NOT BEEN LISTENING

A NOVEL

THE AWAKENING

RON BROWN

TRUSTED BOOKS
A DIVISION OF DEEP RIVER BOOKS

© 2014 by Ron Brown. All rights reserved.

Trusted Books is an imprint of Deep River Books. The views expressed or implied in this work are those of the author. To learn more about Deep River Books, go online to www.DeepRiverBooks.com.

No part of this publication may be reproduced, stored in a retrieval system, or transmitted in any way by any means—electronic, mechanical, photocopy, recording, or otherwise—without the prior permission of the copyright holder, except as provided by USA copyright law.

Scripture references marked NIV are taken from the *Holy Bible, New International Version*®, NIV®. Copyright © 1973, 1978, 1984 by Biblica, Inc.™ Used by permission of Zondervan. All rights reserved worldwide. www.zondervan.com

Scripture references marked KJV are taken from the *King James Version* of the Bible.

ISBN 13: 978-1-63269-232-0
Library of Congress Catalog Card Number: 2013923338

ACKNOWLEDGMENTS

IN WORKING ON this trilogy, I have developed the deepest appreciation for sermons that can clearly be applied to the lives of believers. I am particularly impressed when believers are being taught, through the preached Word, how to become much more resilient in their daily walk. Thus, in the writing of this second novel of the trilogy: *We Have Not Been Listening: The Awakening*, the theme of resiliency echoes throughout the entire work. Using this theme was indirectly encouraged by a very special set of clergymen and clergywomen through their sharing of the redeeming and uplifting Word of God. To them I owe my deepest sense of gratitude.

In this regard, I would like to say thank you to Dr. Rev. Kelly Miller Smith, Dr. Rev. Latisha Reeves, Dr. Rev. Jacquelyn Bragg, Rev. Janice Crawford, and Rev. Fredrick Brabson.

A special word of appreciation also goes to three Spirit-filled women, Mrs. Gwendolyn W. Brown, Mrs. Shirley Carr-Clowney, and Dr. Rev. Jacquelyn Bragg, for their unique words of encouragement and their thoughtful editorial observations.

We Have Not Been Listening: The Awakening

Hezekiah sent to all Israel and Judah, and wrote letters also to Ephraim and Manasseh, that they should come to the house of the LORD at Jerusalem, to keep the passover unto the LORD God of Israel. . . . For they could not keep it at that time, because the priests had not sanctified themselves sufficiently, neither had the people gathered themselves together to Jerusalem. . . . And be not ye not like your fathers, and like your brethren, which trespassed against the LORD God of their fathers, who therefore gave them up to desolation, as ye see. . . . Now be ye not stiffnecked, as your fathers were, but yield yourselves unto the LORD, and enter into his sanctuary, which he hath sanctified for ever: and serve the LORD your God, that the fierceness of his wrath may turn away from you. . . . For there were many in the congregation that were not sanctified: therefore the Levites had charge of the killing of the passovers for every one that was not clean, to sanctify them unto the LORD. For a multitude of the people, even many of Ephraim, and Manasseh, Issachar, and Zebulun, had not cleansed themselves, yet did they eat the passover otherwise than it was written. But Hezekiah prayed for them, saying, The good LORD pardon every one that prepareth his heart to seek God, the LORD God of his fathers, though he be not cleansed according to the purification of the sanctuary. And the LORD hearkened to Hezekiah, and healed the people.

(2 Chronicles 30:1, 3, 7-8, 17-20 KJV)

PREFACE

CHANGE, REAL CHANGE, so I've been told, is seldom gentle. In fact, it is often quite turbulent, causing chaos and confusion. These are, in fact, the atmospherics of the first novel of the trilogy, *We Have Not Been Listening: The Darkness,* in which the characters are experiencing overwhelming stress and trauma. Caught up in the vortex of the Rapture not taken, they find themselves confused, bewildered, and most of all, lost. What does one do when his/her world has been turned upside down? What is one to do when he/she has been displaced, having only a church as his/her refuge? What is one supposed to do when he/she discovers his/her religious activities aren't enough to save him/her? And what is one to do when those he/she loves have disappeared quite mysteriously? These are substantive questions and provocative questions for sure, but they, through the lives of the characters, serve as the vehicle for exploring the purpose of salvation, God's grace and mercy, and the type of relationship we choose to have with our Lord and Savior.

In this the second novel of the trilogy, *We Have Not Been Listening: The Awakening,* God is at work, and the answers to those questions presented in the first novel are being sorted out. For example, with his mentor, G.T. Thomas, the socially-conscious but unbelieving bishop,

We Have Not Been Listening: The Awakening

no longer around to guide him, Carlos Robinson, the associate minister and newly minted pastor of Saint Augustine Baptist Church, must now discover his new calling; Randy Nelson, the gender-conflicted minister of music, who is new to the faith, must find a way to grow in the Lord. Many of the others: C.J., Jo Whitlock, fondly known as 'Sister Minister,' and Steve and Joan are languishing at Saint Augustine Baptist Church, still overwhelmed and still trying to make sense of the crisis in which they find themselves.

My apologies for your long wait. So let's not waste any more time wondering and looking for answers. Let's begin reading and finding out who has made some important decisions and who has not. As always, I wish you Spirit-filled learning.

CHAPTER ONE

"C. J., YOU have been quite the trooper," Dr. Wilson-Ross said, "to have carried this poor girl all the way down here. Thank you ever so much. We will now relieve you of your 'burden,' so to speak, won't we, ladies?"

"Yes, we will," Joan and Sister Agnes chorused together with large smiles on their faces.

C. J. gently placed the young woman on one of the few remaining beds in the infirmary. Smiling at Dr. Wilson-Ross and the other women, he said, "Doctor, she's all yours. See you ladies later on today."

As he began walking toward the door, he heard Dr. Wilson-Ross exclaim, "Oh me, oh my, in all of the excitement upstairs, I've gone off and left my medical bag in the sanctuary. While I don't suppose that anyone would bother it, I'm going to need it . . . now, as a matter of fact." She paused for a few seconds and said, "C. J., I know it's time you were asleep, but would you be a dear and get it for me?"

"No problem, ma'am," C. J. politely said. "Where in the sanctuary did you leave it?"

We Have Not Been Listening: The Awakening

"Well, let me see," Dr. Wilson-Ross said, looking upward as if to visualize where she had left the bag. And then she said, "I think I was sitting near the front of the church . . . probably in the third or fourth row."

"Okay," said C. J., "that gives me better than a ballpark view of where you might have left it, ma'am. I'll be back in a flash." Nodding at them with a smile, he turned and trotted out of the infirmary, heading toward the elevator. It would take him to the corridor on the floor above.

As he moved, he raised his arms and stretched his fingers in an effort to relax them and mused to no one in particular, "That girl didn't initially seem as heavy as when I first picked her up. But by the time I got her to Dr. Wilson-Ross, she felt like she had taken on two hundred more pounds. Women, what do I know?"

He was pleasantly surprised to find that the elevator was still there after pushing the up button, and its doors opened quickly. He entered and pushed the button for the first floor.

Exiting from the elevator, C. J. continued to trot down the long corridor that connected the church building to the Jenkins Family Life Center. Opening the doors to the Narthex, he was some fifteen feet from the sanctuary proper. When he arrived at the sanctuary's double doors, he stopped abruptly. Not only were all of the lights on, but he could make out a figure moving ever so slowly through the thick, yellow-tinted windowpanes of the doors. The figure would stop to bend down for a few seconds, then straighten up and move on to the next pew, as if he or she were searching for something.

His curiosity piqued sky-high, he hurriedly pushed opened the sanctuary doors, and it suddenly became crystal clear who the "mysterious figure" was. C. J. recognized the person as the dude he had met about the same time he had met the late bishop. While not wishing to make any harsh judgments, he had nevertheless taken the dude to be some kind of street hustler.

At the moment, the dude appeared to be on some urgent mission to locate something worthy of his being up at this hour of the morning.

Chapter One

However, upon hearing the sanctuary doors open, the dude froze like the proverbial deer caught in the headlights. He apparently had not counted on anyone else being up and able to disturb his searching efforts. And yet, there was the college kid standing in the doorway.

CHAPTER TWO

C. J. WAS not sure what urged him forward, but he began walking toward the front of the church. He could not come up with an answer as to why or how, but his heart was beating a little faster. Despite his nervous sensations, he was the first to speak. He said, "I thought everyone would be sound asleep by now. Lose something?"

As if jolted by a stiff uppercut, Vince responded by sputtering and stumbling all over himself. "Yeah . . . aah . . . yeah . . . I forgot something . . . so I couldn't sleep, man. It's been a hel . . . er—you know, a rough day and all. But yeah, I left my . . . um . . . you know, um . . . my bag, a little bag. You know, a bag." Gathering himself a little more, he added, "You possibly seen it?"

C. J. was half way down the sanctuary aisle when the other man finished responding to him. There were now just about fifteen pews between them. He took several more large steps before answering the other man. Then he said, "No. I can't say that I have; but the doctor has asked me to retrieve her 'little black bag.' I'm sure that's not the one you're looking for, is it?"

It wasn't so much the question itself that Vince again found jarring but the insinuation that he might be doing something he shouldn't. He paused a minute or two, valiantly trying to recover himself from this perceived accusation. The momentary delay on his part allowed C. J. to move within five pews of him. As C. J. did so, he spied Dr. Wilson-Ross's medical bag one pew over, leaning against the arm of the pew nearest the side aisle. Taking what amounted to a running broad jump, C. J. landed at the pew containing the doctor's bag, leaned down, and snatched it up. Sticking the bag under his left arm, he sighed, feeling relieved that he had accomplished his mission: locating and securing the doctor's medical bag.

His self-satisfaction was short-lived. The reason: a scowling Vince was staring at him, now just two pews away. Despite his rapidly beating heart, C. J. chose to ignore the dude's angry expression as being a personal threat. He said hastily, "Well, I've got what I came for. It was a little careless of the doctor to have left her bag just lying here, eh? But you're right—it's been a long day. I'll get this back to her, and then I'll get some shut-eye, eh? Good luck with your search, man."

Seeing his opportunity about to slip away, Vince spoke quickly, "Hold up, bro . . . er, let's talk about your little find there. Um, if the truth be told, that's the bag I was looking for. You know what I'm saying? The doc is a nice lady and fine too, but she don't need to know that you've found her bag. You know what I'm saying?"

There is nothing like putting it right out there, C. J. thought. *This admission from the dude confirms my initial suspicions about him. I shouldn't be too surprised; it's not like I don't know people like him exist. In fact, there are dudes just like him in my neighborhood and around the school I attend, Fisk University, just hanging out, not going anywhere, and not doing much with their lives. They seem primarily interested in "getting over" any which way they can. Sadly, this focusing on meeting their own needs tends to obscure the consequences of their actions—to others as well as themselves.*

While C. J. was reflecting on the ins and outs of the dude's character, morals, and motivation, the dude had moved from being two pews away to standing directly in front of him in the center aisle. "Man," C. J. said under his breath when he saw the dude standing in front him and blocking his exit, "Was he that fast, or did I just space out?"

This observation was quickly followed by much more alarming thoughts. *Fight? Am I going to have to fight this dude in order to protect the doctor's bag? He's a little taller than me and a bit slimmer, but I have a few pounds on him so I might be able to hold my own. But why? It doesn't make any sense. I'm just a preppy, nineteen-year-old college kid with a youthful expression, and he looks so street-hard, he could be twice my age.* This line of thinking immediately provoked the rapid beating of his heart to the degree that it felt like it could come through his chest!

Attempting to dismiss how he was feeling, his mind returned to the notion of having to fight. *I had had only one fight in my entire young life, and that was actually more of a scuffle. I and another third-grader had gotten into a wrestling match, on the grassy lot adjacent to our elementary school, over who would be first in the school lunch line. Fortunately for us, some of the teachers were fairly close by and quickly intervened before either one of us was seriously hurt. The only casualties of our confrontation were scuff marks on one of my shoes and a partly torn right sleeve on my new athletic jacket. The other kid, however, had a red welt under his left eye, but that was it.*

At the time, however, this kid's status paled in comparison with how my parents reacted to our scuffle. My father, a Methodist minister, had very little patience for roughhousing, let alone fighting, and he most certainly did not approve of me being involved in any such activity. The physical price which I had had to pay still lingered in my memory banks.

While this situation was entirely different, he was hoping to avoid a confrontation, so C. J. extended his hand and said, "I'm C. J., and I didn't catch your name the other day when you arrived at the church."

CHAPTER THREE

IGNORING THE OUTSTRETCHED hand, Vince shot back, "Let's cut to the chase college boy. The doc has stuff in her bag that I need, and understand that I need it now! She doesn't have to know that I have any of it—plain and simple! We can forget all this introduction stuff 'cause I know you! Oh yeah, I know all about you. You're the kind that does what he's told; so now do what I'm telling you to do!"

Great, C. J. thought as he listened to the dude, *I can't finesse my way out this mess! This is so crazy! How in the world did I get myself into this dumb situation anyway? I was just trying to be a stand-up guy, someone that folks could count on . . . now this. Am I going to have to fight this dude . . . in church of all places . . . to protect this bag? You know, God, this being your house, I'd like to think that you'd have some opinion about what's taking place here.*

Sliding the razor out of his back pocket, Vince yelled, "What's it gonna be, college boy? I don't have all morning. Either do something or get off the pot!"

C. J. wasn't quite sure where his words came from, but they came nevertheless. He said, "So let me get this straight, my brother. You want me to give you the doctor's bag so you can get high? Am I breaking it down right, my brother? That is, after all that has taken place in the past twenty-four hours or so—people mysteriously going missing, the bishop dying of who knows what, and we're having to hold up here with no place to go—to have you ask me to become a co-conspirator in, of all places, God's house. Is that where you're coming from?"

Frustrated by the other man's reluctance to promptly comply with his demands, Vince snarled contemptuously, "God's house? Fool! Don't be so naïve! God's house is full of pimps and whores! That's all they are, them church folk—you know, minister, deacons, Sunday school teachers, just fancy names for frauds and cheats . . . all of them steal and stuff. They're just like the rest of us. They're no better, worse even . . . because they try to act so holy!"

Vince paused for a few seconds, hoping that his little speech might persuade the college boy to see things his way. Then attempting to sound conciliatory, Vince flattened out his voice and said, "Look, man, I just need a taste. Just a little something. You know what I'm saying? After that you can give the bag back to the doc. I don't care. I just need something to tide me over!"

For some reason, C. J. hadn't seen it before: that is, the razor the dude was holding down at his side. Perhaps it was the dude's earlier confrontational tone which distracted him. Seeing it now told him that he had run out of time, and he needed to do something quick because at this hour of the morning, with everyone asleep, he was in this situation all by himself. So he thought to himself, *I could tell him I'm a "P.K."* *(Preacher's Kid), but he'd just laugh me to shame. Maybe, just maybe, God will hear a prayer from the likes of me.*

So as loudly as he was able, he began praying, "Heavenly Father . . . I can't claim to be your most obedient servant. As a matter of fact, I'm probably in the same class as Gideon, the least of the least and the worst of the worst. I'll understand if the words I utter don't make it above the tops of the pews, if that high. But merciful Father, I would ask, yes, beg and plead your grace on me and the dude here. As you can plainly see, neither of us has been straight with you or with anyone else. So please forgive us . . . "

Before C. J. could add another word or even say amen to his prayer, Vince harshly cut him off by yelling, "You think that God's gonna jump down here and save your punk rear end? And if there's a God, you think he's got time to worry about either of our sorry butts?"

Raising the razor so that it was now in plain view, Vince continued, "I'm tired of talking, chump! I'll cut you so bad that it'll take a lifetime to make you look halfway decent. Now give me the bloody bag!"

CHAPTER FOUR

DR. WILSON-ROSS LOOKED down at her watch and said to the two women, who had accompanied her to the church's clinic to attend to the formerly distraught young woman, Rachel Anderson, "It's nearly one forty-five! Where could C. J. be after all this time?"

Joan, who was eager to please, said, "He's young and undoubtedly not very time conscious or maybe the new minister needed his help . . . to lead him to the bishop's study. You remember that we just left him standing there when we all hurriedly exited the sanctuary. He certainly looked like he could use some help."

"I hear what you're saying," Dr. Wilson-Ross said, "but that was almost forty-five minutes ago. I guess if you want something done right, you have to do it yourself. Just keep an eye on her, please. I'll be right back!"

Just as quickly as she began moving toward the door, she stopped and said, "What size shoe do you wear?" Joan looked first at Sister Agnes and then down at her feet. Looking up, she said, "Oh me, I wear a size six, why?"

"That's good, I also wear a size six, and these boots will only slow me down on my way up to the sanctuary and back. Can I borrow your tennis shoes, please?"

Chapter Four

"Well, I've loaned out blouses, skirts, and dresses, but never tennis shoes. This is most definitely a first. Now I should warn you that I've been in them most of the day, soooo, I can't promise that they will be in the best shape, if you know what I mean?"

"I've got a small spray bottle of Escada in my purse," Dr. Wilson-Ross said, smiling, "if you feel that I'll be overwhelmed. But I'd really get worried if after wearing them, my feet shrunk down to a size three."

"I don't really think they will be that bad," Joan replied, laughing along with Sister Agnes as she removed each of her tennis shoes. "Just try not to scuff them up too much. They're just a few weeks old." Once she had them off, she handed the tennis shoes to Dr. Wilson-Ross.

"I'll be extremely careful," Dr. Wilson-Ross said, smiling, and proceeded to slip on the tennis shoes that didn't require shoelaces. "They fit just fine. Thanks, again. I'll be back."

Turning abruptly, she quickly made her way toward the exit and out into the corridor. She darted down the partially lit hallway to the elevator. Once there, she pushed the first floor button several times, as if this would make the elevator's doors open any faster. After they opened at their regular speed, she hopped in and quickly pushed the first floor button. When the elevator arrived at its destination and the doors opened, she leaped out and ran towards the Narthex.

Once there, she noticed that the double doors to the sanctuary were closed, but she thought she heard voices coming from inside. Moving closer to the doors and peering through their small glass windows, she was able to make out the owners of the voices: C. J. and Vince.

Besides the raised voices she heard, her eyes caught the light flashing off of something Vince was holding in his raised left hand. He was gesturing wildly with the other. When he raised the left hand higher, she knew immediately what he was holding in his hand. It was a razor, and he was threatening C. J. with it.

"But why would he do that?" she said aloud to no one. "Could it be about whatever C. J. is clutching in his arms? Dummy! I know it's early, but C. J. has my bag . . .my bag—my black bag! Vince is after my

11

bag! He must be after the meds . . . more specifically, the opiates in the bag. I was willing to give him the benefit of the doubt when we first met and not make any snap judgments about him, but he must be an addict for sure! C. J. is protecting my bag from Vince, and he could be killed!"

CHAPTER FIVE

IMPULSIVELY, SHE WAS about to barge into the sanctuary when
something stopped her. As fast as this impulsive feeling hit her,
another crucial thought struck like lightning. It basically told her that
despite providing medical services in an inner city hospital, she was
out of her league in this situation. She was in no position to take on
a street-smart drug addict with a razor in his hand! She was going to
need help for sure!

"But who?" she asked herself and then added, "Of course, the new
minister. He is the closest. I better move fast. I don't know what that
crazy Vince might do to poor C. J."

She stepped quietly away from the sanctuary's double doors and
started to make her way in the opposite direction from where she had
come. But she stopped abruptly, uncertain about whether she was
headed in the right direction. First looking left and then right, she
saw an intersection down the hallway. She began trotting again in the
direction of the intersection. Once there, she was pleased to discover that
Saint Augustine had, what could only be called, excellent signage. She
was met with two signs, one pointing east and the other pointing west.

She squeaked, "Thank you!" as she read the sign that pointed in the east direction. That sign read, "The Bishop's Study." The other sign pointing west read, "The Church Library" and "The Church Secretary's Office."

She took off running, as fast as she could, down the east corridor in the direction of the bishop's study. She stopped when she reached the only doorway at the end of the corridor. The door had a medium-sized brass sign above it that read, "The Bishop's Study." She knocked respectfully but lightly as if observing some proper protocol. Hearing no response, she knocked again, only this time much harder. Initially, she heard what appeared to be some rustling inside, and after a few minutes, that was followed by a deep voice saying, "Hold on a minute. I'm on my way."

Then she heard the sound of footsteps being methodically placed. Finally, she heard the latch being undone, and the door to the bishop's study was opened. Dr. Wilson-Ross found herself standing face to face with the new minister of Saint Augustine, the Reverend Carlos Robinson.

The corridor's lights were dimmed, she presumed as a cost-cutting measure—given the early hour of the morning. Nevertheless, she was able to make out his features from the light coming from the study. He was a little over six feet tall with short, black, curly hair, high cheekbones, a straight nose, full lips, and a strong chin. His complexion was a medium tan, and this along with the other features she observed, strongly suggested that he must be the product of mixed heritage. He was wearing a navy-blue robe with white piping around the collar and cuffs over light-blue pajamas that had the collar turned up. Black suede slippers covered his feet. Her observations were interrupted by his deep yet mellow voice. "May I help you?"

Upon hearing him speak, her heart skipped a beat or two. Shocked at this surprised reaction on her part, she quickly chided herself by saying, *You've seen him before . . . why this reaction now? So he's attractive . . . and fine—I do mean fine! Even at this early morning hour. Get ahold of yourself, girl! You already know the scoop on him! Get a grip! Do what you came for!*

He asked again, his voice a little stronger, "May I help you? You have to excuse me . . . I'm not able to make you out, but if you tell me what's troubling you, perhaps I can be of some assistance."

She wasn't quite sure how she missed his eyes. *It must be the low lighting here, she thought. Anyway, they seem to have a cloudy, white substance covering them. It's like the type of thing you see when someone loses their sight as a result of developing cataracts. Something must have happened since their initial encounter. At the time, he had been able to see well enough to have brought that young woman minister to the church. No time to ask what happened or even to examine him. Need to deal with that craziness taking place in the sanctuary. I've already wasted too much time!*

She said, "Your presence is sorely needed in the sanctuary right away. That miserable little man that your former pastor brought here is threatening dear C. J.—with a razor!"

"Well then," Carlos said as he stepped into the hallway, "we better get a move on." Extending his right hand, he said, "Your elbow please." He took hold of her waiting elbow and they were off in the direction of the sanctuary.

Carlos quipped, "Sorry we can't do a forty-yard dash, but this fast walking should get us there in no time at all. By the way, I'm Carlos Robinson, the new minister at Saint Augustine. Whose elbow, if I may ask, do I have the privilege of holding?"

"Oh, so sorry . . . I'm Dr. Wilson-Ross, that is Dr. Chandra Wilson-Ross, and we met when you brought your colleague in . . . um, the young woman minister who was in the car accident. I'm so sorry . . . in my haste to get you to the sanctuary, I hadn't noticed that . . . um . . . well, you know, I wasn't aware of the difficulty you were experiencing with your vision, Reverend."

Chandra slightly shrugged, thinking to herself, *What else could I do? Better to lie than to say I hadn't been paying attention during the earlier church service. I'm not a religious person, so I was checking my phone messages prior to the little girl passing out. Now what I am going to do with a blind preacher and that crazy situation in the sanctuary?*

"Let me put your mind at rest, Chandra, if I may be so familiar," Carlos said. "We're up to the task. And by the way, did anyone ever tell you, ma'am, that you could have been a world-class diplomat? To tell you the truth, losing my sight came as a major shock to me as well. I can assure you this sightless thing takes some getting used to. Perhaps when things settle down, you can take a look-see, as it were, doctor."

That's weird, please don't tell me he can read minds now, she told herself. "Why of course, and no I don't mind," she said and added, "here we are at the sanctuary. Let me get the door, okay?"

"By all means, do," Carlos responded.

CHAPTER SIX

THE ABRUPT OPENING of the lower level sanctuary door startled Vince, who was holding his razor high above his head, looking as if he was just about to cut C. J. But seeing Carlos and the doctor enter the sanctuary, Vince let out an epithet under his breath and told himself, *It has hit the fan, bro, but you got to play this hand out now. There's no going back and no choice about this deal now. They got to know that you're no punk!*

He had no sooner expressed this bit of bravado when he heard the sound of the double doors open on the upper level. Because of the light that poured through them from the Narthex, he initially wasn't able to make out the two figures standing in the doorway. When they moved inside the sanctuary, he immediately saw Shadow and another man, whom he did not recognize at first. Taking a quick second look, he knew this other man to be Steve! Quickly recalling his earlier confrontations with both of these men, his heart jumped several beats, and he thought, *My hand has suddenly changed quite a bit, and it ain't good; that's for sure.*

C. J., on the other hand, was having a radically different reaction to seeing the sanctuary doors swing open, below and then above. He whispered, "This is your house, God, no doubt about it! Thank you, Lord! Neither of us is worthy, Lord, but thank you for being here!"

Attempting to talk himself back into his hard and defiant posture, Vince made his face into even more of a scowl and snarled, "Don't even think that their coming in here is going to save your butt, college boy! I want what's mine, and I aim to get it. I don't care who's around. Now don't make me ask you again. Give it here!"

C. J. remained silent, but he did not move as much as an inch. He thought, *Though I walk through the valley of the shadow of death, thou art with me . . .*

Carlos asked, "How far are we from C. J. and the other young man who is trying so hard to be some kind of gangster?"

Chandra replied, "We are about ten or maybe twelve rows, or should I say 'pews' from where they are standing. If I thought you wouldn't fall or injure yourself, I'd suggest we jog to about where they are."

"Sounds like a great idea, doctor," Carlos said. "Why don't we?"

Off they went, shoulder to shoulder. As they jogged, Carlos said, "Let's stop when we are just about to reach them, say a pew or two away. Okay?"

"That's fine with me," Chandra said. "I just patch them up. I'm not in the 'saving business,' if you get my drift."

"Hmm," Carlos said smiling, "Sounds like when I'm finished working out the problem that these two young men are having, you and I will need to have a chat."

"I wouldn't spend too much time," Chandra quipped, "focusing on my soul, Reverend. Because believe me, you have a much larger problem on your hands at the moment!"

With about four pews to go, Carlos and Chandra slowed to a trot, and they heard, "I knew you were up to no good from the moment I saw you, punk! That's all you are, just a little punk!"

It was Shadow, shouting from the upper level of the sanctuary. He was hoping to distract Vince from doing what he was planning to do since he and Steve were too far away to actually intervene. He had no idea that his shout out would have any possibility of freezing Vince's efforts to hurt C. J., but in fact, it did just that. In any other situation, at any other place, and at any other time, Vince would have surely cut C. J. But this wasn't an ordinary place, and it wasn't an ordinary situation, and most assuredly, it wasn't an ordinary time!

CHAPTER SEVEN

"**A**RE WE ABOUT there?" asked Carlos as they slowed to a fast walk.

"Just about where you want to be," replied Chandra.

"Fine," said Carlos. Then in a loud voice he said, "Everyone stay where you are." After pausing for a few seconds he continued, "Now young man, how important is your life to you?" Flashing through Carlos's mind just as he was asking that question was, *I know what happens when you're disobedient to God . . . I've lost my sight and the bishop lost his life. Maybe, just maybe, I can help this young man.*

Initially startled by the young minister's voice, Vince closed his eyes to gather himself and then yelled back, "That's a dumb question, preacher. It's very important! What's it to you? You gonna save my soul? Some preacher! What, you all holy now? I know all about you . . . the big lady's man! Screwing everything with a skirt on, be she tall, short, fat, or thin, it don't make any difference! You can't tell me anything! All you can do, man, is to stay out of my way and out of my business!"

"Wrong, my young brother," Carlos said. "You're God's business and that makes you my business. He has great plans for you . . . that is, if you choose life . . . and there isn't much time for you to make that decision."

"Cut the bull," Vince yelled back. "You don't believe that crap any more than I do. Haven't you heard, preacher, God helps those who help themselves . . . and I'm about to help myself! Now back the hell off and leave me alone . . . you Jack-legged preacher!"

"It's not God's will or way that anyone should be lost, son," Carlos said calmly as he pulled away from Dr. Wilson-Ross's elbow and moved towards Vince.

"Are you sure you want to do that?" Chandra asked in a voice slightly higher than normal.

"If he's not offered a chance to discover God's redeeming love, then he might never know that it is real. He really doesn't have to make the same mistake that I and the bishop did!" Carlos responded sharply.

Her voice even higher now, clearly reflecting both doubt and fear, Chandra asked, "Given his deluded state of mind, do you think there is any chance of that?"

Carlos did not respond to her, but taking one step at a time, moved ever closer to Vince. As he did so, Vince struggled to shout, "Didn't I . . . tell you . . . to . . . stay away?" Quite mysteriously, the muscles in his throat had tightened up, making it difficult to speak.

As Carlos continued to move even closer, Vince tried to take a swipe at him with his razor, but once again, here was something else he could not do. His arm would not move, no matter how hard he tried. This sudden challenge to speak as easily as he was accustomed to doing along with the difficulty of moving his arm, made his heart beat extremely fast. His inability to control what he previously had no problems controlling produced a level of fear the likes of which he had never experienced.

While he was trying to assess and analyze his sudden physical losses, he was also being urged to decide with alacrity whose side he was on! He heard Carlos urgently say, "There isn't much time, son. You need to decide now if you're on God's side or your own."

In addition to these problems, Vince also sensed his legs beginning to stiffen up. This caused him to sway back and forth as he struggled to maintain his balance. The combination of these physical losses with his heightened level of anxiety caused him to cry out, "What's . . . happening . . . to . . . me, man? Oh, man . . . Oh, man! What's wrong? Oh, man . . . help me! Please, oh, God!"

To those watching this drama unfold, it was plain to see that Vince had become completely immobile. He and the famous "Tin Man" could have been kissing cousins, he looked so stiff.

When Carlos stopped walking, he was within an arm's length of where Vince was trying to maintain his balance, and he could have easily touched him if he had chosen to do so. Taking advantage of his close proximity, Carlos asked again, "What will it be, young man? I assure you, you do not have even a minute to spare! Now it sounds like you are having problems putting words together, so a simple 'yes' or 'no' will do. Quickly now, for as I've said, you don't have very much time! In fact, you have just about run out of time! What is your decision?"

Vince did not waste time pondering his decision. He figured that whatever had happened to him during these last several minutes was only going to get worse, and he wanted no part of that possibility. So straining as hard as he could, he forced out, "Y . . . e . . . ah! Man, yeah!"

CHAPTER EIGHT

HEARING VINCE'S RESPONSE, Carlos said, "I will assume that you totally and completely understand the decision that you've made this day. There will be no margin for error or room for any memory lost, now or in the future, my young brother, should you want to change your mind."

Then Carlos reached out his right hand so that his fingers initially made contact with the back of Vince's head. They slowly moved to the top of his head until they reached his forehead. Once there, Carlos began to pray, "To the all wise and most powerful God, Whose love and mercies endure forever. Only You can turn the old wine into new, and only You can make that which was ripped and torn, whole. Have Your way with this young soul, Lord. Show him the magnitude of Your love, grace, and mercy. And grant, if it is Your will, that his sins be forgiven. In Jesus' name, the name that is above all names, I pray this prayer. Amen."

Save for the heavy breathing from all of those present, an anticipatory stillness came over the sanctuary as Carlos finished praying and withdrew his hand.

Relieved that he was still in one piece, C. J. was nevertheless awestruck by what was now taking place; but he wondered, *How is God planning to answer the young minister's prayer?* His wait, and that of the others, was neither long nor in vain, because ever so slowly, Vince's body began to twist and jerk. To the small group watching, it appeared as if a very strong electric current was passing through his body—from the top of his head to the tip of his toes. Whatever was happening was mysterious and took somewhere between fifteen and twenty minutes. When it stopped, C. J. marveled at the results, which were quite remarkable.

At first blush, Vince appeared to be completely restored to his former self. However, upon closer inspection there was one significant difference. This involved the right side of his body. Starting with his head, there was now a distinct sagging on the right side of his face that included a drooping of his right eyelid. As a result, one could barely see his right eye. Next, his right arm hung listlessly, and the fingers on his right hand were grossly disfigured.

Chandra was the first to react to what she saw, "Oh my, oh my . . . I'm not sure . . . that there will be much I . . . can do. . . ."

Her bleak and brief observation was followed by Shadow's bewilderment. "Saaay! That's messed-up, man! How could that happen?"

C. J., anxiously running the fingers of his right hand through his short-cropped hair, said under his breath hoping not to be heard, "I know I've messed up, God, but please don't allow that to happen to me. Please!"

Steve turned away, choosing not to see what stood in front of him. He said nothing, electing to keep his thoughts to himself.

These comments initially did not register with Vince, who had no way of seeing the changes that had taken place on his face and torso. But when he attempted to stretch the fingers on his right hand and tried blinking the eyelid over his right eye, his brain quickly moved into action. It reported back with alacrity that various parts of his body were now dysfunctional! This was more than he could handle, and he cried out, "Whaaat's happen . . . ing . . . to me? It's not . . . faaiiir, it's not . . . riiiight! I did whaat . . . you asked me . . . to . . . do. Not faaaaiiir!"

CHAPTER NINE

CARLOS STEPPED CLOSER to Vince and placed both of his hands on his shoulders. He said softly but firmly, "You did say yes, did you not? And you are still alive! God heard your plea and that's why you are still here, alive! Now He wants to see what you will do with the gift that He has given you—*life*!"

"Life . . . life . . . like this?" Vince sputtered angrily.

Carlos responded with a tone of frustration in his voice, "Did I stutter, my young brother? That's what I said, life! God chose to spare your miserable, little *life*. He chose to give you one more chance, and not only you, my brother, but all of us!" Pausing to simmer down a bit, Carlos then continued, "We're all in this sad mess because we've not been listening! Let me break it down for you, son! I lost my sight because I thought I was smarter than God! Fortunately, because of His grace and mercy, He is not finished with any of us yet! Hallelujah! Otherwise, we would all be goners. Glory to God!

"Now before it's much too late to get any rest whatsoever, would whoever is here besides C. J. and the good doctor assist our young brother to the Family Life Center and to bed?" Carlos then said, "Wait! Please wait. It must be my poor upbringing, but I would so much like to know the names of the others who are here to share my thanks. So if you would, please take a minute or so to share with me who you are to have assisted us at this early hour of the morning."

Shadow was first to respond, and he said, "The name's Shadow, and I'm kinda like a night-owl. I was wandering around your church. It's big, man, is it big—when I ran into Steve coming this way. Look, I'm here because the late bishop asked me to help him get some of the folks who were stranded because of the craziness taking place out there to your church, here. He even let me drive his Mercedes, can you believe that? Anyway, I knew when I first saw this thug that he was up to no good; and I told the bishop so. We should've left him under the rock he crawled out from!"

Steve responded next and said, "My name is Steve, and . . . uh . . . I've lost my wife in all that mess out there. The late bishop invited me here in the hope that we might eventually find her. Now I'm not so sure we will, and because of that, I haven't been able to sleep very well. The ladies in the clinic told me that the nurse was up here. I ran into Shadow and— Sorry about that . . . you didn't ask for all of that. We'll see that he gets back up to the Center, Reverend."

Carlos said, "I'm not surprised that you each met the bishop in the ways that you have. He was forever reaching out to others, seeking whom he could help in an effort to improve their lives. He believed that to be his calling, his mission. He was nevertheless a man like you and me, with faults and failings; but he had a decent handle on judging character."

He sighed and continued, "You know he would be there for you regardless of the horrible trouble you got yourself into. I'm here because of the interest he showed in me. So Shadow, I wouldn't be so hard on the brother; we all need a little grace now and then.

"And Steve, there's no reason to be sorry, for I share your sense of loss as well. My prayers for you, the others who are here, and I include myself as well, are that we will make positive use of this time, and above all else, that we understand the grace God has afforded us. Now let me

26

thank you gentlemen again for your help and support, and I wish you a good morning."

Shadow nodded at Steve, and they both stepped forward like two Russian guards, one on each side of Vince. Steve removed the razor from Vince's disfigured fingers and gave it to Dr. Wilson-Ross. Initially surprised by this "gift," she nevertheless took it and put it in her black bag. Vince thought to say something objecting to this sudden liberation of his weapon, but given his newly limited physical condition, he decided against it. They took Vince by his arms, lifted him up, and began walking toward the rear of the sanctuary. Vince, already anxious from what had happened to him, initially attempted to resist, but the firmness of their grips quickly told him that resistance was futile. Relenting, he let himself be half carried and half dragged towards the double doors.

But for the intermittent sounds coming from Vince's tennis shoes dragging on the carpet, there was silence in the sanctuary. Within a few minutes, the silence was again broken by the sounds of doors opening and then closing.

Of the three who remained, Carlos was the first to speak. "On reflection, doctor, it occurs to me that perhaps our young brother should have the benefits of a medical person to briefly examine him prior to putting him to bed. Therefore, he would be better off at the church's infirmary rather than going to the Family Life Center. If it is not too much to ask, would you be so kind as to catch up with the guys and redirect them? I think it is best that he be under your professional and watchful eye. Okay?"

"No problem," Chandra said. "I've done all-nighters earlier in my medical training, so another one now shouldn't matter. I just hope that we won't have anyone else requiring medical assistance. That little infirmary of yours is about full to overflowing. By the way, I also hope that you are giving some thought to what needs to be done with the remains of your late pastor—er—it is only right that he be buried . . . and buried quickly, if you get my drift."

"Loud and clear," Carlos said sharply. "Loud and clear."

Chandra then turned her attention to C. J. and gently said, "Thank you, my knight in shining armor, for being so protective of my little black bag. You are indeed a gentleman and a dear friend." She quickly leaned over and brushed C. J.'s right cheek with her lips. She smiled at him, turned with her black bag in hand, and began trotting off toward the rear of the sanctuary.

Reacting as though he had just experienced the ninth wonder of the world, C. J. exclaimed, "Wow! Man! She's some woman, ah, I mean lady! She smells good, too. Oh, I'm sorry, reverend. I didn't mean . . . to go off like that. It's just . . . ah . . . "

Carlos chuckled and said, "I can't say that I actually witnessed what just took place between you two, but whatever it was, I just hope you are back in touch with terra-firma enough to assist me to the bishop's study. And my nose also tells me that she's wearing an exciting brand of perfume. Shall we go, my young friend?"

CHAPTER TEN

A**S THEY CASUALLY** walked in the direction of the bishop's study, C. J. was the first to speak. "Um, I'm glad you guys, I mean you, Reverend, the doctor, Shadow, and Steve, arrived when you did. No telling what Vince might have done . . . all over a little black bag. I can't believe it, and I was there. I have to thank God, too, because I was sure praying that He would intervene, and He did, wouldn't you say? That poor guy looks awful and—"

Cutting in, Carlos observed, "C. J., I'm pleased to hear you were praying. But I'm also hoping your prayers weren't mainly asking God to make like He was a 'fire-escape' of some sort. Instead, I'm hoping you were praying from a deeper realization that God, as the author and finisher of our faith, is in the midst of everything happening to us. So I trust that while you were wanting for Him to rescue you, you had a deeper objective in mind and were profoundly motivated in your request. That is, you were after a deeper relationship with Him! Then despite the outcome between you and Vince, you would still have been in great shape!"

"So I guess I still need to do something about my relationship with God if I completely understand what you are saying, Reverend?" C. J. said glumly.

"Paul, the apostle, said, 'For me to live is Christ and to die is gain.' So when you have an ongoing relationship with God, C. J., you're in a win-win situation, my young friend," Carlos said, smiling.

"I guess so," C. J. said, still not totally convinced by the logic of Carlos's reasoning. They continued to walk, lost in their own thoughts, and after several more steps, C. J. said, "Well, here we are, Reverend. Let me get the door, sir."

Once they were inside the bishop's study, C. J. directed Carlos to the late bishop's leather desk chair. Once Carlos seemed settled, C. J. said, "Rest well, sir." And he began making his way toward the door. Just as he was about to exit, Carlos called out to him, "What time is it, C. J.?"

C. J. responded, "It's a quarter to two, sir."

"I 'm thinking we'll need to get an early start on the day, C. J. So if you can stop by for me around eight, that would be good. The bishop's suite is great as a central location to the rest of the church, but it's not where I keep my things. So I will need you to run by my suite and pick up some items for me. Here's a set of keys, and this small key is for the elevator. When the key is inserted and turned to the right, then you can press the button for the floor above this one. My suite is the first one to the left of the elevator and has my name above the door. If you would be so kind as to bring back fresh undergarments, socks, a clerical collar, shirt, and a pair of black slacks, I'd appreciate it." Carlos added, "Thanks. Try to get a few good hours of sleep . . . we'll have much to do later on. Okay? "

"I will," C. J. said. "You too, sir. Thanks again and good morning." With that he stepped through the doorway and headed toward the hallway intersection.

Wearily, Carlos leaned his head back against the large, leather chair. Feeling reasonably comfortable, he placed his two hands behind his head and said aloud, "I don't know how You are marking down this day in that big, old book of Yours, Lord. But I've got to tell You, well, I mean . . . you know what I mean to say. Just that it has been some day . . . with the bishop gone . . . and I trust that he is now with You. But, I'm not sure how You expect me to fill his big shoes. And Sister Minister...after her terrible van accident…with that piece of glass sticking out her forehead… she's . . . almost gone . . . My prayer is that You'll see Your way to allow her to stay around here. It's just that I could surely use the help with the spiritual and administrative things she does so well. In fact, she should be here rather than me.

"Now I know it sounds like I'm feeling sorry for myself, but Lord, You got to know I'm out of my league. I suppose this is not news to You—it's just me who needs to remember. Okay, enough about me, Lord, I'm also needing to pray for the young woman You blessed earlier with a sense of peace and a willingness to seek Your grace and mercy. Of course, I can't forget the young brother whose life You spared just a few minutes ago. I don't know the reason You gave him his life back, but I know that like the rest of us, he was surely on his way to hell. So I've got to know that You have kept him here for a special purpose. Allow him, Lord, to come to that understanding real soon.

"Lord, this is quite a congregation You have blessed your servant to shepherd. Give me the wisdom, Lord, I pray, the knowledge, the understanding, and the patience to lead and minister in a way that gives You the glory and honor. Thank You. In Jesus' name, Amen." When Carlos finished praying, his arms came down, his hands fell to his lap, and he drifted off to sleep.

CHAPTER ELEVEN

MIDWAY UP THE center aisle, Chandra quickened her pace, and by the time she reached the double doors, she was coming through them like a halfback hitting the defensive line. Just looking at her, no one would have thought she was so fast and agile. At five-five, she was wiry but filled out in all the right places. At first blush, with her first lady's features, look-alike hairstyle of bangs and shoulder-length hair, one might have been dubious. But once she was out in the Narthex, barely breathing hard, all doubts would have been quickly diminished as she began making her way toward the corridor where the elevator were located. She mused to herself, "Given all the running that I've been doing this morning, it's a good thing that I've taken my own advice to stay in shape. Those early morning workouts I've been doing surely have come in handy this morning. Now I better get a move on if I'm to catch those gentlemen before they reach the elevator."

She lengthened her strides as she picked up her pace. She told herself, *This isn't much different from running those four by four relays when I was on the Tennessee State University women's track team. Although that was several years ago, I remember that I often had to make up some time, so Rykia, who was running the anchor leg, could make it home for the win.*

Chapter Eleven

Striding along easily, her mind quickly shifted to what she had just witnessed. She said softly to no one in particular, "Vince's recent behavior surely makes a case for us to view him as a low-life, which is both tragic and sad. I knew that he was streetwise, but he seemed so pleasant and reasonable at first. One can only wonder how well the others will relate to him now, once they hear how horribly he behaved.

"But it was his take on the young minister that, if I didn't know better, would have made me even more annoyed with Vince. What can I say? I've heard those very same things before from a number of my female patients. So I know he has this weird effect on women . . . as indicated by my own reactions earlier." She giggled, slightly embarrassed by her behavior, and continued, "Stupid and very much like a schoolgirl—guilty as charged—your honor. But I also have to say, womanizer or not, the brother most definitely took charge of that situation—and he's blind, too. You can be fine, but you have got to handle your business; and I've got to give him credit for that. He took care of business in spades!"

She paused for a second or two, sensing that her emotions were getting too far ahead of her more rational side. To put the brakes on, as it were, she thought, *Now hold up here, don't get too excited, girl. Besides his sordid reputation, he is also into that God-thing. You're a physician and your gods are science and medicine. There's got to be hard evidence for what you do and believe. And now a sister also has to be careful with all these make-believe preachers carrying on in the church building—not that that's a worry of mine. As I've said, I'm a scientist, a doctor; I'm a 'just the facts' type person, and mysticism just isn't my thing. But if I'm being honest, I have to confess that something out of the ordinary happened in that sanctuary. With all my medical training, I do not have a rational explanation.*

As she approached the corridor where the elevator were located, she heard voices and surmised that they must belong to Shadow and Steve. To be sure they would hear her, she shouted, "Hey, gentlemen, wait up. There's been a change in the plans."

CHAPTER TWELVE

"HERE'S THE ELEVATOR . . . say, isn't that the doc's voice?" Steve asked.

"Sure sounds like it," Shadow responded. "We better wait and see if we can be of any further assistance."

"I see her now, and she is moving at a fast clip. I'd thought she'd be dead tired . . . they've had her going since she arrived. She didn't get a minute to even catch her breath. She's definitely a warrior, for sure!" Steve observed.

Vince had been sulking and silent prior to reaching the elevator. Now he spluttered a not so veiled sexual comment, "A warrior . . . I'm not . . . too sure . . . but she is fiiiine. I'd . . . like to baaattle with heeerrr. If . . . youuu get . . . myyy . . . meannn—"

"Boy!" Shadow shouted, "I've just about had enough of you and your foul mouth. I'm this far from snatching you up in here. It don't matter if we're in church or not!" He glared at Vince. Before he could utter another word or take a step closer, Steve had stepped between him and Vince.

Taking a sideways glance at Vince, Steve said, "Isn't it strange how someone is always stepping in to save your rusty backside? First it was the bishop and now it's me! Me, you hear me! Me, the husband of the woman whose car you stole. I'm stepping in to save you! I sure hope the minister was right about you still being here because of some unknown reason that only God knows!"

Turning back to look at Shadow, he said, "Believe me, Shadow, I know how you are feeling. I really do, man. But we just finished, you know what I'm saying—just finished having some craziness a little while ago. Do we need any more drama at this hour of the morning? Aren't we—you and I—better than that? Come on, man. Look at him! You and I both know that if he were really man enough—and not a child masquerading as a man, then surely he would not have gotten himself into this peculiar mess—and certainly not in a house of worship! I'm not an overly religious person, but I got to think that whatever higher power—or God, if you will—one chooses to believe in has already dealt with him and done so quite severely if you ask me, Shadow!"

"I don't know if I could have put it that way, that well, but you're probably right, man," Shadow said. "It's just that punks like him make my blood boil with the things they try to do and say. But I'm good, for sure; I'm okay now . . . and no need losing it over some worthless piece of . . . Oh, here's the doc. Was she saying something about a change of plans?"

Having slowed down to a fast walk but breathing heavily, Chandra approached the three men. Holding up her left hand before speaking, she leaned over to catch her breath for a few seconds. Then bolting straight up, she said, "Everything okay here? I thought I heard what could best be described as animated voices." She looked at each man for an answer.

"We're good," Steve replied. "You said something about a change of plans, did you?"

"Well, first off, thank you for waiting, gentlemen," Chandra said. "And that's right—um, the minister suggested, right after you left, that it might be better if I took a quick, preliminary look at Vince to make certain his breathing and heart are still in good order. Thus, rather than taking him to the Family Life Center, we need to go to the church's infirmary."

Once again, seeing that neither of them had any reaction one way or the other, she said, "Shall we be on our way?"

Shadow nodded affirmatively and pushed the down button.

CHAPTER THIRTEEN

C. J. THOUGHT, *I'm too hyped up to head directly toward the Family Life Center, and I wonder what's down that hallway.* Upon reaching the intersection, he continued walking straight in the direction of the church's administrative offices. He was hoping to find one of them open. He was feeling the need to reflect on what he had just been through and wanted a quiet place to sit and ponder.

Not surprising at this hour of the morning, each office he encountered—the community outreach, the business, the Sunday school education, the secretary's, and even the mission's office—was locked tight. He was about to make the trek back the way he had come when he noticed a light coming from what appeared to be yet another office not far from the mission's office. He took several more steps and found himself standing in front of it. It turned out not to be an office as he had surmised, but a small chapel. In fact, it was the staff's chapel according the sign above the doorway.

The chapel door was opened and the lights, low and mellow coming from inside, gave off a warm and inviting feeling. As C. J. stepped just inside the doorway, he was met with what he thought was a pleasant aroma of rose petals, orange peels, and cinnamon sticks. Whatever it was, it made him feel even more comfortable.

We Have Not Been Listening: The Awakening

As he moved forward, he determined that the chapel was an oval-shaped room with a center aisle and four long pews on each side. The pews' upholstery was decorated in a floral design of light tan and maroon. The walls on each side were also light tan but windowless. Each one had four mid-sized, neatly-spaced, framed paintings depicting some of the healing miracles that Christ had performed. Up front, he could make out a carpeted, round, double-stepped platform covered with the tan and maroon floral design. The platform had a very large podium in the center made of polished mahogany. On the curved wall above the podium hung a large, multicolored, stained glass depiction of a shepherd and his flock.

After pausing to take in the particulars of the chapel, C. J. walked slowly down the center aisle and plopped down on the first pew to his right. He slumped forward and rested his head against the back of the pew. He closed his eyes and slowly began a pictorial review of what he had been a part of not too long ago.

This time, he thought, *I will be a spectator and not a frightened participant.*

The images flowed quickly until he reached the one where he saw himself praying; then all of a sudden, they stopped. He opened his eyes and said softly, as if he did not wish to disturb anyone, "The minister was right. Look at me, frightened out of my wits and just throwing out words. Repeating what I've heard over the years. I had no idea what I was saying or to Whom I was saying it. That was rude. I was rude. It's like expecting my father to give me the keys to the family car when I haven't done anything he has asked me to do. And here I was asking God to help me, and I haven't done anything He has asked me to do!"

His eyes began to well up with tears as those earlier hopeless, helpless, and gut-wrenching feelings began to return. Along with them were the accusatory thoughts that although he was a P.K., he was basically someone who could fool some of the people some of the time with his "knowledge" of the Word. But in reality, he was no more than a hypocrite, a religious charlatan, and, in plain language, a basic phony!

This combination of feelings and thoughts triggered a torrent of tears from what had initially started as only a trickle. The volume of his voice went up a little higher as he cried out, "I know now that . . . oh, God . . . You've come . . . taken those . . .who were faithful, Lord. I'm so . . . sorry!"

Sobbing loudly now, he continued, "And you know, I'd thought that . . . I'd have . . . a little more time to get to know You, Lord—you know, get closer. Oh, God . . . to You! That I'd be . . . a much older man, you know, like the folks in my father's church. But given the last fifteen hours or so, it looks like the proverbial clock has struck twelve . . . and I've . . . run . . . out of time. Jesus!"

Pausing briefly to collect his thoughts and to remember what had just happened with Vince, he cried out loud, "But You . . . You spared the dude just a little while ago . . . Lord, is it too late . . . (sob) for me to . . . make amends? Oh, God, if there's . . . still time, you know . . . a few minutes more . . . even a few seconds more—Jesus, I'm Yours!"

C. J., with his eyes still closed, gradually became quiet, his heavy sobbing given over to intermittent sniffling. He sat there waiting, not sure for what, but waiting. After several minutes had passed, hearing nothing, feeling nothing, he slowly opened his eyes and began wiping the tears from them.

When he had finished, searchingly he looked around the small chapel, hoping to see something, anything to tell him all hope wasn't lost. Sadly, he was still in relative darkness save for the several artificial candles stationed on both walls of the chapel. However, it wasn't until he began focusing on the front of the chapel that it became evident that everything was not as it had been before. This is when he noticed the light glowing above the podium on the platform.

Intrigued, C. J. slowly got to his feet and began making his way forward. He was now about five feet from the podium. His movements resembled those of a person in a trance, and he took each step toward the podium, as if he were on a tight rope.

When he finally stood behind the podium, the glowing light was still there. In fact, the light was coming directly from the open book resting on the podium. The book was the New International Version of the Bible, and it was open to the book of Revelation, chapter three, verse twenty. This verse appeared to shine even brighter.

We Have Not Been Listening: The Awakening

He read, "Here I am! I stand at the door and knock. If anyone hears my voice and opens the door, I will come in and eat with that person, and they with me." These words were barely out of his mouth when, with eyes closed and head bowed, he sank to his knees. He whispered, "Yes, Lord, I most certainly want You—now! Thank You for Your forgiveness, love, and mercy. Thank You, Lord. Thank You for Your precious Word!" He remained in that posture for some time, continuing to give praises for God's many blessings.

CHAPTER FOURTEEN

W HEN CHANDRA, SHADOW, and Steve arrived at the church's infirmary, Joan and Sister Agnes were still there. From the expressions on their faces, Chandra knew they would have at least one hundred questions or more, so she quickly said, "Ladies, I do apologize for keeping you waiting for what has already been a long day. Sadly, as if we did not have enough excitement yesterday, Vince, one of our very own, thought he would add a little more. So, in an effort to quiet him down, as you can see, we were forced to bring him to the infirmary."

After getting that preliminary explanation out of the way, she directed Shadow and Steve to take Vince to the last remaining examining bay. Once they were there, without being told, they lifted Vince up, with Shadow taking his upper body and Steve gathering up his feet, and placed him on the examining table.

Complaining, Vince attempted to say, "Whaaat . . . are . . . you going to do . . . to . . . meee?"

"Not to worry," Chandra said, following quickly behind them. "We're simply going to make sure you sleep well. If I recall correctly, you earlier had something in mind to calm your nerves, isn't that right? Well, this I believe should do just fine."

"Hoooww . . . you know whaaat . . . I waaant?" Vince yelled and struggled to free himself in an effort to move off the table. Unfortunately, his nonfunctioning limbs made that endeavor difficult, along with Shadow and Steve, tightening their grip on him, told him that he wasn't going anywhere.

All the while, Chandra was standing by with a needle in her gloved right hand and a cotton swab dabbed with alcohol in her left. She said, "Would you roll up the sleeve on his right arm, Steve?"

"Certainly, ma'am," Steve replied.

Rubbing Vince's upper arm with the swab, a frowning Chandra gave Steve a stern look. Then smiling, she said, "Save 'ma'am' for your mother or grandmother. Doctor will do just fine, thank you." After tapping Vince's arm three times with her left hand, she injected the needle she had been holding with her right.

Vince let out, "That . . . hurt—" This utterance was shortly followed by the rolling of his eyes up toward his forehead, then slowly closing them and slipping into a deep sleep.

Chandra said, "That should hold him through the rest of the morning, gentlemen. So once again, thank you for your kind assistance. Go get some rest while it is still dark out there."

Waving them off, she turned to the two women and said to Joan, "If you'll hand me my bag off that table, I can take care of Rachel, who has been resting while I had to attend to Vince.

"We didn't have much to do while you were away," Sister Agnes observed. "She fell asleep right after you left. We were grateful for that, but I can see that you surely must have had a time of it with that one."

After retrieving Chandra's black bag, Joan chimed in, saying, "I'm not one to judge, but when we first met him I knew there was something odd about him . . . that rang of being un-churched. You know what I mean? The way he spoke and the way he was dressed. He struck me as the typical street person caught up among church folk. So I guess I'm not surprised that his true colors finally came out. I'm so glad we weren't there to see him act a fool because he must have been more than a little crazy up there, wouldn't you say, Dr. Wilson-Ross?"

"Given the hour of the morning, permit me to give you ladies just the *CliffsNotes* version by saying it was very, very interesting indeed. But now, after I give her this shot to enable her to sleep restfully, we can all go and get some sleep ourselves, all right? Once again, thank you very much for your assistance, and I do apologize for having you wait so long," Chandra said.

Then she quickly opened her black bag and withdrew in the following order: a small blue packet containing an alcohol cotton swab, a small bottle containing a cloudy liquid, and a small syringe. Tearing open the blue packet and removing the cotton swab, she rubbed her young patient's bare, right arm. After drawing what was the needed amount into the syringe, she injected it into her.

"This should keep her resting soundly through the remainder of this morning," Chandra shared. After placing a plastic cap on the syringe and putting it in the red plastic container above the bed, she returned the other items to her bag. Then reaching for the light-blue blanket resting on one of the small tables nearby, she opened it and gently covered her young patient with it.

"Ladies, I think we are done here for the time being," Chandra said. Smiling at the two women and gesturing toward the exit, she said, "Shall we take our tired bodies to bed?"

CHAPTER FIFTEEN

A S C. J. exited the elevator and began making his way toward the
Family Life Center, he was still caught up in the exuberance of
knowing his sins were forgiven and that he was now, without a shadow of
a doubt, a child of God. As he walked, he was quietly saying to himself,
"Thank You Lord, thank You, Jesus, thank You, Lord."

He was instantly jarred out of his trance-like state by the sound of
someone calling his name. He looked to his right but initially did not
see anyone. Then he heard again, "Over here, C. J."

He looked to his left and saw Shadow standing near a partially opened
door. With his face upturned, he appeared to be blowing something from
his mouth. He had no sooner finished making that gesture when he drew
something to his mouth and then quickly flicked it away. He stepped
back inside from the partially opened door, allowing it to close. As C.
J. drew closer to where Shadow was standing, he smelled the residue of
cigarette smoke.

Shadow spoke first and said with a snicker, "You're just getting
back from the bishop's study. It must have taken quite a bit to get the
preacher all tucked in."

C. J. studied the man for a few seconds, not believing what he had just heard him say. He thought, *Shadow must have been smoking some very strong stuff, and he shouldn't have been smoking in or near the church in the first place! He must know that and also know that I'm aware of that fact as well. Where is he coming from with a crazy question like that? Lord, I figured that it would be a little while before the testing came, but here it is, up close and personal.*

While C. J. was reflecting, Shadow continued his barrage of questions with, "How does it feel to be like a rat in a maze, running from the doctor to the preacher and from the preacher to the doctor? It's got to be tiring, wouldn't you say? And I know you were peeing in your pants when that boy was about to cut you with his razor. I know you were scared out of your ever-loving mind, weren't you? You had to be as glad as a pig in slop when we all showed up."

C. J. looked down for a few seconds, and in that amount of time, he prayed, "I know what I'd normally say to such a stupid man, but You wouldn't be glorified in that. Give me the words Lord that You would have me to say." He looked up, paused, and then said, "You're up late, Shadow, and don't you think it's also a little late for twenty questions? As for the minister, my guess is that he's probably sleeping, which is what I plan to do now."

With that, he proceeded to make his way toward the Center, As he did so, Shadow stepped in his pathway, blocking him.

Shadow said, "Boy, you didn't answer my questions. You think you're pretty smart. Just the nice, little, helpful, college boy. You can't fool me."

C. J. stepped back a little bit to give himself some breathing room. Looking directly into Shadow's eyes, he said with the deepest conviction he could muster, "You asked, was I scared? Yes, I was scared, no doubt about it; but you were there. You saw what I saw and heard what I heard, but I'm guessing you did not feel what I felt. Yes, I was scared then; but now I have no good reason to be afraid of anything, or for that matter, anyone!"

We Have Not Been Listening: The Awakening

He paused for a second or two to let his words sink in and continued, "There's no doubt in my mind, Shadow, that God was on full display earlier this morning, and we got the chance to experience Him up close and personal! So if there are any questions to be answered, you should be concerned about the ones He has for you!" With that he pushed passed Shadow and continued on his way.

Shadow's tendency for things to be either right or left, up or down, black or white was one of his failings. As a result, he could easily become intensely angry when things did not go the way he felt they should. Thus he said to no one in particular, "Did he just push past me like he wasn't scared of me? Me, and I outweigh him by a 150 pounds or more! I know that Vince, as well as some of the others here, are scared of me, but this kid, he didn't even seem scared of me! Why not? I could beat him to a pulp. I ought to run and grab him, snatch this smart-mouth, know-it-all, college kid up!"

These words had barely cleared his mouth when, all of a sudden, he paused for a few seconds as if he had just had some sort of epiphany. This gave rise to his sounding a little less sure of what he would do, and he said, "But you know . . . something about his face . . . really more his eyes . . . seemed to be saying . . . not now, maybe not ever. Hmm. Whatever it was, I'll tell you this: it wasn't there before this morning!"

With the image of C. J. growing smaller and smaller as he proceeded down the hallway, Shadow also felt his anger beginning to subside a little more and a little more. As a result of this, much to his surprise, he began to feel lonely and unwanted. These despondent emotions forced him to ask, as if he were speaking to someone who would be interested, "Where was the bishop when I, Shadow, needed him most? We had gotten along so well after our initial misunderstanding. The bishop saw value in me; he showed me that I was needed, and that gave me a purpose.

"Now with the bishop dead, who needs me? Is that it? This college kid has replaced me, and I've been kicked to the curb. Is that why I'm so angry? Stop it! This is only taking you back to places you don't want to go. Before the bishop asked for your help, you didn't know him or these folks and then that simple woman smashed into your Escalade. So stop sweating them. Who needs these people anyway? If you have to worry about anybody, you need to be worrying about your own family. Since all that mess started out there, you haven't checked on them in a while. Keep your priorities straight and forget these folks! You probably need to be getting in the wind anyway and moving on."

With that concluding thought, Shadow turned in the opposite direction of the Family Life Center and headed toward the kitchen. He said aloud to himself, "I wonder if they left any snacks out?"

CHAPTER SIXTEEN

SWEATING, WIDE-EYED, AND with his nose flaring, Steve sprung up from his cot. Grabbing his chest with his right hand, he felt his heart pounding away at ninety miles a minute, or so it seemed. The rapid heaving of his chest told him that his breathing was also coming fast and furiously.

"What . . . is . . . going . . . on . . . here?" he asked no one in particular. "What's wrong with me? I . . . need to get up and out of here. Hard . . . to breathe . . . could be having a heart attack. Got to get some air . . . can't stay . . . here!"

Tossing his sheet and covers aside, he swung both legs over the side of the cot until his feet found the floor. Using both hands and arms to lift himself, he pushed upward off the cot. Standing but swaying, he lunged forward in the direction of the double doors, some fifteen feet away. Stumbling as he did so, he crashed into one of the small end tables with an unlit lamp on it belonging to his nearest neighbor.

His nearest neighbor, in the cot some four feet away, happened to be C. J. He had, not too long ago (perhaps thirty-five or forty minutes), dropped onto his cot and attempted to snuggle up to his pillow in an effort to go off to sleep. Were it not for Steve's anxious behavior, crashing into his end table, C. J. might have been moving toward some REM sleep.

Instead, he was awakened quite suddenly by the lamp falling on his right shoulder. Rising up, he said, "What's going on? What in heaven's name is happening here?" Seeing the lamp that had fallen into his bed, he pulled it's small chain, and the light revealed a figure awkwardly making his way toward the double doors. Holding the lamp up higher to give him a clearer view, C. J. recognized the short salt and pepper hair, the white-collared blue shirt, and the dark blue pants. Of course, it was Steve!

He called out, "Steve, what's wrong? Are you sick?"

A foot or two away from the double doors, Steve, using as much energy as he could muster, yelled back over his shoulder, "Got to . . . get . . . out . . . got to . . . get . . . some air!" With that he threw himself at the double doors, pushing them wide open. The muted light that poured into the darkened room, along with the earlier commotion, was sufficient to wake up a few others, including Randy and the older deacon. They both asked, as if in a Greek chorus, "What's going on? What happened? Is someone sick?"

C. J. said, "It's Steve. I think something is wrong with him. He went stumbling out of the room into the hallway saying he needed some air. You think it's a heart attack?"

"Let's not get too far ahead of ourselves," Randy said. "But to be on the safe side, why don't you go for the doctor, and I'll see about Steve, okay?"

"Sure," C. J. replied. "I can do that."

"What do you want me to do?" asked the deacon.

"Just hold down the fort here, sir. We don't need everybody out in the hallway creating more confusion. But thanks for your willingness to help out," Randy said.

"We're all servants," the deacon said. "All servants."

With several of the lamps on now, including his own, C. J. was able to find his tennis shoes, put them on, and begin trotting toward the double doors on the far side of the large room. As he moved, he thought, *Gee, I'm supposed to get the doc. But I don't even know what room she's staying in. I guess I'm going to have to wake up several of the women. I hope they won't be too unhappy with me. I'm doing it for a good cause.*

CHAPTER SEVENTEEN

BY THE TIME Randy had his tennis shoes on and had moved to the other side of the double doors, Steve was nearly down the hallway to the elevator. Randy called out, "Hey, Steve, wait up."

Steve called back, "I'm not . . . sure . . . I can . . . go much further . . . so what else can I . . . do but wait?"

Finally catching up to him, Randy asked, "Where in the world were you headed, Steve, at this time of the morning?"

"I'm . . . not sure," Steve said. "I just knew . . . that I . . . needed . . . to get . . . out . . . of there; that I needed . . . some fresh . . . air. In fact, I'm still . . . feeling a little shaky. My heart's still . . . pounding . . . and I can't . . . seem to breathe . . . evenly. I don't know . . . what's wrong with me . . . all of . . . a sudden."

"Not to worry, the doc is on her way," Randy said. "You know, sometime back, I used to do some certified nursing assistant work on a part-time basis. They showed us this little deal to help with getting your breathing back. So while we wait, let's try this, okay?"

"Sure," Steve said. "Anything . . . if it . . . allows me . . . to . . . breathe better."

Randy began to lift his arms ever so slowly, holding them up for the count of three, and then lowering them again. He repeated this several times, encouraging Steve to imitate what he was doing. As Randy did so, he inhaled when he raised his arms and exhaled when he lowered them. Randy did several more of these arm reps and asked Steve, "How are you doing? Feeling any better yet?"

Steve said, "Um . . . it's strange . . . but yeah, I'm slowly getting back to feeling sort of okay. I'll do a few more until the doc gets here. By then, I should be back to my old self, I hope." He was about to say something more when he saw the doctor walking quickly toward them. He said, "Here's the doctor now." Randy turned to see the doctor and C. J. approaching.

When they arrived where Randy and Steve were standing, Chandra said, "Who is the patient, if I may ask?"

Steve said, "Sorry to get you up, doc, knowing that you haven't gotten very much sleep, but I'm the 'patient.' I woke up with the jitters, sweating, dizzy, heart running wild, and on top of that, it was difficult to breathe."

Chandra said, "What you are describing sounds very much like a panic attack. Any idea what might have triggered it?"

Steve, frowning and with a strong tone of incredulity in his voice, said, "I can't say that I know what could have 'triggered it' as you say. I don't usually have 'panic attacks.' In fact, I don't believe I've ever had one before now."

"Don't get yourself in a dither Steve," Chandra said. "Your manhood is still intact, as far as I know. But you're an educated man, so you must know something about the research that says anyone, male or female—you included—can have, will have, either an anxiety attack or a little ole 'panic attack' at some time in his or her life."

"I know enough about the research, doctor, to know that I don't fit the typical profile for someone having a panic attack!" Steve said sarcastically.

Chandra didn't respond; she simply opened her little black bag and took out a small bottle. After removing the bottle cap, she poured two small, white pills into the palm of her left hand. Turning and giving the pills to C. J., she said, "Please don't call me again unless you have an actual emergency on your hands. Good morning." She put the cap on the bottle, returned it to her black bag, winked at C. J., and quickly headed back toward the Family Life Center.

The three men stood looking at one another, hoping that one of them had an explanation for what had just taken place.

C. J. was the first to snap out of his little fog and said, "I'm guessing these are for you, Steve," and he handed him the two pills. He turned slowly in the direction of the Family Life Center, then stopped and said, "I hope you get to feeling better, Steve. You should know the doctor is a good person, and we are truly blessed to have her here."

Without another word, he turned back and walked slowly toward the Center.

CHAPTER EIGHTEEN

SHRUGGING HIS SHOULDERS to express how perplexed he was, Steve looked at Randy and said, "People are a bit touchy this morning, aren't they? I mean, I'm the one who was maybe on his last breath; you'd think I'd get some understanding. But I didn't really need somebody telling me who I am, like I'm some kind of pu—"

"Punk. Is that the word that you're looking for?" Randy said sharply. "Is that what you're so upset about? That someone might be thinking that you're not man enough, Steve?"

"Hey, man, er . . . look, Randy, I meant no harm. I spoke out of turn. Sorry. Okay? Look, you helped me and I'm really grateful. But I've never been in a situation like this before. Like I told the doctor, I've never had one of these things before. And I . . . "

"Hey, my brother," Randy said, "I remember now, you missed it upstairs; I'm not where I was some twenty-four hours ago. God has taken charge of my life, and what seemed so essential before is no longer essential at this time. You know, it just hit me, Steve—just maybe God is trying to get your attention with this 'thing' as you call it. And you probably know this already, but the research does say if you've had one, you could easily have another. So unless you like this feeling, I would do something about it ASAP. But for now, I too hope you get to feeling better. Now you should take the pills and try to get whatever sleep you can."

He was about to turn away when Steve said with a sense of urgency in his voice, "Hold up, Randy, what were you talking about when you said I needed to do something about how I was feeling a few minutes ago, ASAP? I'm going to take these pills the doctor gave me, and that should make everything all right, shouldn't it?"

"Let me cut to the chase here, Steve," Randy said, sounding a little annoyed. Then catching himself, he softened his delivery, "My guess is that until you straighten out what ever triggered that panic attack, you are subject to having others. It is as simple as that, man. Something you did or didn't do is messing with you; and this place is no place to leave it unfinished. By this 'place' I mean God's house, okay? Now I'm going to get some sleep. I'm sure the new minister will have stuff for us to do later on."

Before he could take a step or two away, Steve blurted out, "You're right, I did miss whatever you shared with folks upstairs, and I'm sorry about that. So what that means is that neither of us knows how we came to be at Saint Augustine, right? Well here's the deal, Randy. My wife, Mia, has come up missing, and I'm worried sick that something terrible has happened to her. And I also believe that Vince may have been involved with her disappearance, since he was driving her car. Now the late bishop stopped me from hurting the little fool and brought me here with the hopes of finding out what might have happened to Mia. Earlier this morning when I had this 'panic thing,' I was dreaming about her. She was being raped, and I couldn't help her, man. I couldn't help her, you hear me! I couldn't help her! But the rapist, the dude who was doing it, he was laughing at me! It was like I was there, but I was basically invisible to what was actually taking place. It was a weird, sick dream, you know?

"Earlier in the evening I was okay, but that was before Shadow and I arrived at the sanctuary and saw what was taking place there. You know, it was seeing that street kid again, Vince, going through his craziness that brought it all back. I can't keep going through this heavy guilt thing. I just can't. I know I messed up, had an affair, but it's all over now. I promise you that it's truly over."

"Straight up, Steve," Randy said. "Here's the deal, as you like to say. God is able. God is able to overcome anything and everything we've done or will ever have to deal with. Now I'm not promising you that Satan won't mess with you over this thing you did. Just like I know he will try to mess with me about my sorry history. But God has a plan to deal with him and with what you did . . . whenever that was. What you need to decide here and now is whether you're ready to let Jesus Christ come into your life. What do you say? Like the minister said, 'Time is not on your side.'"

"Is that all I have to do, man?" Steve asked.

"It is just a short and direct prayer, Steve. It goes like this: 'Jesus, I'm a sinner who is lost. I ask Your forgiveness for all that I've done. I accept You as my Lord and Savior. Thank You for Your love, Your mercy, and Your grace. Amen' Do you think you can handle it, Steve?" Randy asked.

"I already have. I was following along as you were sharing what I needed to say. Look, again, thanks for hanging in there with me. I know I wasn't very pleasant. I was rude to you, the doctor, and even to C. J. You were all trying to help me. Sorry, man. I'm really sorry. Hey, man, I know that I kept you up a bit, so why don't you go on ahead. I'm too wound up to get any sleep now. I think I just need to find a Bible, if there's one to be found around here. Thanks again, man. Good morning, Randy."

Randy extended his hand and said, "No problem, man, but there are plenty of Bibles here. The late bishop made certain of that. When you get upstairs and walk to the intersection, you will see a sign pointing west on your right. Take it as far you can, and you will come to a small chapel. In there, you will find a Bible, for sure. Good morning to you as well, Steve."

CHAPTER NINETEEN

DESPITE ALL OF her efforts to quietly slip into the suite she was sharing with Joan, before she was actually inside, Chandra heard, "Is everything okay with the guys? Who was the 'sick little boy' this time? These men are always fronting off like they're so strong and everything. We girls are going to have fun with whoever it was. So, girl, who was it? You know we're going to need his name if we're to do this thing right."

Sensing that she no longer had to tiptoe into their suite, Chandra closed the door tightly with a small thud and placed the safety chain on the door, allowing it to clang. She entered the area that served as their living room and found Joan. She was sitting in the king-sized, white-cushioned chair in her short-sleeved, full-length, black, silk nightgown that covered her drawn up knees and feet. She was smiling and eagerly awaiting a response from Dr. Wilson-Ross.

Looking at her, Chandra thought, *She's so hyped up, you would think we were at some sorority rush party or something. I'm a bit too tired for that sort of nonsense, and I'm in no mood for a girls' all-night talk fest.*

So she said, "No one was actually sick in the true sense of the word; one of them was having difficulty getting to sleep. Everything is okay now." She paused and then added, "I told them not to call me again, unless the Center was drifting off into outer space . . . and not even then. Good morning, sweetie."

Before Joan could utter another word, Chandra had dropped her black bag on her bed and was very gracefully lying down beside it. In the few short seconds it took her to do that, Chandra was fast asleep.

Hmm, Joan said to herself. *This is the second time that she has done me that way—just cut me off like I'm some two-year-old or something. Rude! She's rude that way! She's the big doctor, and everyone else is below her! This is not quite finished yet . . . not by a long shot. Oh, well, after all the commotion, I'm not going to be able to go back to sleep now. And since she won't talk to me, maybe I'll go for a little walk. That should tire me out, and then I can go to sleep.*

She picked up her silk, rose-colored robe and slipped it on over her nightgown. As she did so, she thought, *Walking around like this shouldn't be a problem. Not this early in the morning. . . and not in a church at that!* She slipped on her black tennis shoes, stood up, and walked to the door. She removed the safety chain and quietly opened the door. Before leaving, she briefly looked at her suitemate, made a face, and then stepped into the hallway.

CHAPTER TWENTY

O N HIS WAY to the church's intersection, Steve passed by the kitchen and noticed that the door was ajar and the lights were on. While this scene slightly piqued his curiosity, he decided not to stop and check on it, thinking, *It is probably one of the old church mothers trying to get an early start on breakfast,* until he heard the sound of a pan crashing to the floor and a deep voice loudly emitting an expletive.

This caused him to stop suddenly because he was now several feet beyond the kitchen. He thought, *No one said anything about locking this building up, so anyone could have come in. We're sleeping . . . at least most of us . . . and whoever that is, is burglarizing the place!* He turned and ran back toward the kitchen. Much to his surprise, when he pushed opened the kitchen door, Shadow was standing in front of the stove, waving his left hand.

Steve said, "Shadow, what happened?"

Shadow said, "I was hungry, and I thought I would fry me up some eggs, but I got the pan too hot, and it slipped out of my hand. I burned my hand, too. It's gotta little sting between my thumb and forefinger. I guess I better go and see the doc about it."

"I'm not sure that's a good idea, Shadow," Steve said.

We Have Not Been Listening: The Awakening

Frowning, Shadow said, "Why not? Isn't that what she's here for, to help the sick and the injured?"

"It's not a good idea because, first of all, it's nearly five o'clock in the morning. And secondly, given that she was just here to attend to one of you poor little babies, she's probably fast asleep by now and not wanting to be bothered by anyone. That's why."

Both Steve and Shadow spun around to find out who the owner of the disembodied voice was. Much to their surprise, there was Joan, standing in the doorway with arms folded and a stern expression on her face. The annoyed quality was still in her voice as she said, "Don't look surprised; I didn't expect to see you either, and I didn't think anyone would be up this early! And as I said, she was just over here looking after one of you little boys. But she wouldn't tell me who the poor little lamb was. I don't suppose it was you, Shadow. She would've taken care of it. Let's see your hand."

Shadow looked at Steve and then looked awkwardly back at Joan. He seemed uncertain about what to do. Exasperated, Joan raised her voice and said, "Look, minister, I'm not the doctor, but I've seen plenty of minor burns before. And don't worry, I won't bite you. Bring your little ole hand here for mama to see it, honey. And Steve make yourself useful by getting some ice cubes from the refrigerator and putting them in one of the dishtowels hanging over there."

Sheepishly, Shadow walked slowly over to where Joan was standing and extended his left hand. Taking his hand in hers, Joan looked it over and saw the redness on his thumb, his fore-finger, the small area between the two, and the tip of his middle finger. She touched the area lightly, and Shadow nearly jerked his hand away. Still holding onto his hand, Joan said, "Now there's no doubt that it's a little tender, is there, Shadow? Steve, have you finished wrapping those ice cubes up? The poor man is in agony."

Instead of doing what was asked of him, Steve brought over a half full ice tray and a floral-patterned dish towel and placed them on the counter where Joan and Shadow were standing. Disgustedly, Joan looked at Steve, sucked her teeth, and said sarcastically, "Men, what are you good for?"

She let go of Shadow's hand, leaving it hanging. She opened the towel to spread it as wide as possible and then emptied half of the cubes onto the towel. She arranged the four ice cubes so that they would lie flat, folded over the dish towel to enclose them. Twisting both ends of the towel, she placed it on Shadow's hand and knotted the ends.

"There," she said, "that should hold you until the doctor has a chance to look at it. Look, if you're that hungry, there are oranges and apples in that basket on the counter near the door. As sure as I'm standing here, the mothers of this fine church have a menu in mind for the breakfast they plan to serve. And they are not going to take lightly, you two messing around in their kitchen! So get a piece of fruit and go! You hear, go on."

Once again, looking like two little boys caught with their hands in the cookie jar, they walked slowly over to the basket near the doorway. Steve had thought to respond to this mistaken accusation, but recalling that he needed to keep his distance from Joan, he decided against it. He simply took the first piece of fruit his hand grabbed and went on his way. Shadow, clutching his injured hand to his chest, looked despairingly at the fruit and decided against taking any, choosing instead to hold onto his injured hand. Slowly walking behind Steve, he followed him out into the hallway.

Joan watched the two men move down the hallway and then turned to see what items needed to be put back in order. She turned off the burner that Shadow had attempted to use. She took down one of the padded gloves hanging near the stove. Putting it on, she reached down for the frying pan that Shadow had dropped when it burned his hand. She placed the frying pan back on one of the three unused burners and replaced the glove on its hook. She walked to the doorway, turned off the lights, stepped into the hallway, and closed the door.

We Have Not Been Listening: The Awakening

She said to no one in particular, "That's enough excitement for one night. I'm most definitely ready for bed." She began making her way back toward the elevator.

CHAPTER TWENTY-ONE

"SHE PUT US out like we were some kids in one of the classes she teaches or something. She's a real piece of work, isn't she? Say, come to think of about it, isn't she a teacher at the school where you're a principal, Steve? I mean, she seems to know you well enough to call you by your first name and all," Shadow said.

"Um . . . yes, she is. She is a colleague and one of our many fine teachers," Steve responded.

"Well, you know, man, I just like to check things out because I don't want to step on another man's territory. You know what I'm saying?" Shadow observed.

Steve abruptly stopped walking and paused to study Shadow, who was about a foot or so away smiling at him.

After a few seconds, Steve said, "I'm not quite sure where you're going with this, Shadow, but I assure you there's no 'territory' in question here. As you may recall, when I first met you and the late bishop, I was trying to find my wife, who is now among the missing. Nothing has happened to change my mind about finding her!"

"Easy, man," Shadow said. "Nashville's a large city, to be sure, but our part of it is like a very small town. People talk, that's all. Miss Joan is fine as all get out, and it would be real hard for a brother in his right mind to miss all of that, you know what I'm saying?"

"Hearing you talk, Shadow, I would have thought that you just arrived. But you have been here the last eight or so hours, just like I have. Nothing is what it was, man, nothing! Whatever was is no more; gossip, all of it means nothing. I'm not the same man I was a little over an hour ago; so whatever you heard isn't worth the smelly breath that passed it on to you, Shadow!" Steve said sternly.

The tone of his voice a bit softer, Shadow said, "Steve, Steve, we're friends, right? I'm not saying that I believe all that stuff. I'm just being straight up with you, man. You know, since you two are both here, I just thought I'd check things out, like I said."

"I guess I haven't made myself very clear," Steve said. "I do apologize for that. Now a little over an hour ago, I became a Christian. Yeah, that's right; I accepted Jesus Christ as my personal Savior and became a Christian! So while I'm still new at this faith thing, whatever was in my past is all behind me now, Shadow. And I was on my way to find a Bible when I stopped to see what all that commotion was about in the kitchen."

"A Christian . . . a Bible . . . I'm dumbfounded. What are you telling me, Steve? How did that happen? You had a good thing with Miss Joan; can't see how you would have given her up so lightly, man." Shadow said, looking quite perplexed.

"Shadow, to put your mind at rest, here's the long and the short of it. After that incident with Vince, I had a very bad dream that involved my wife being raped and my not being able to help her! This dream really unnerved me, so much so, that I guess, according to the doctor, I had a panic attack. Yeah, I'm surprised, too. But anyway, while I was waiting for her to get to me, Randy did some maneuver that essentially calmed me down. And . . . "

"Randy! Randy did what to you, man?" Shadow exclaimed loudly.

"You're way out in la la land, Shadow. All he did was to have me wave my arms up and down, like this. I don't know where you're going, but

---

---

that simple procedure seemed to do the trick; it helped calm me down. When the doctor arrived, all she had to do was to give me some pills."

"I'm confused, Steve," Shadow said. "What does all of that have to do with you giving up one of the finest black women in the world, my brother?"

"I grant you, Shadow, that she is a very attractive woman, no doubt about it. But the decision I made a little while ago is about more than just getting a piece, Shadow! It had to do with *obtaining peace of mind!* And no one, man or woman, was going to be able to give that to me. This may surprise you, Shadow, but it was Randy who clued me in on the fact that only Jesus the Christ was capable of giving me that comfort, that peace, and that forgiveness. I took him up on his word. That's the whole story, Shadow."

"You're right about that, Steve," Shadow said. "Some story, all right, a heck of a story, but um . . . well, look, I hope you find your Bible and stuff. I should be getting back. I'll holler at you later on, man." Shadow turned and began running back to the elevator.

Somewhat stunned by Shadow's reaction, Steve mused, *Well, I guess I shouldn't be too surprised at Shadow's behavior. Yesterday I probably would have behaved the same way if someone had tried to share his or her faith with me. Mia, yes, Mia tried ever so hard to do just that, and I tuned her out. What a fool I was. I didn't know when I had someone special! Now she's gone! Lord, I hope Randy's right about You forgiving fools and sinners like me. I sure hope he's right. I couldn't go on if he was wrong. Please be right, please forgive me, Lord.*

CHAPTER TWENTY-TWO

J OAN WAS HALFWAY to the elevator when she thought she heard what
sounded like someone running and running her way fast. She stopped
walking, momentarily, to confirm what she was hearing. *That is someone
running, and he or she is rapidly coming this way. Dressed the way I am, maybe
I'd better start moving quickly to the elevator,* she thought.

Half walking and half running, Joan arrived at the elevator in no time
flat. Breathing heavily and holding her chest, she leaned against the wall
nearest the elevator. Just as she began reaching over to push the down button,
she heard the heavy footsteps come to a complete stop. She turned slowly
to see Shadow leaning over, trying to catch his breath. He was gesturing to
her, but it wasn't clear what he needed or what he was trying to get her to
do. Then the elevator arrived.

Surprised, Joan wasn't sure what she should do. As she tried to make
up her mind, Shadow said in a voice that sounded like someone had put
his throat in a vice grip, "Hold the door, please."

What else can I do? she thought. *I'm trapped and I'm dressed like this!
Wait, I could take the stairs and get away from who knows what.*

Before she knew it, Shadow was standing alongside of her, saying, "I
got it; go ahead, ladies first."

Chapter Twenty-Two

Once they were in the elevator, Shadow, breathing heavily and his voice a little deeper, exclaimed, "Twice in one night, Ms. Joan. You saved me twice in one night. That has to be some kind of a record, wouldn't you say?"

"If you say so, Shadow; now if you would push the down button, please, we could be at the Center before the sun comes up."

"I like the way you talk, Ms. Joan, like there's a melodic ring to your voice. As for the sun coming up, you're not thinking we're some kind of vampire-like creatures or something, are you? But if the truth be told, I do believe we are different from these folks. Seems like everybody here is becoming a Christian, or so they say. That is, except you and me. Did you know that just this very night, your friend and mine, Steve, became a Christian? Can you believe that? Steve of all people when he had such a good—and I do mean a good thing going? What do you think about that, Missy?"

"First of all, I'm thinking," Joan said, "how do you know that I'm not a Christian? And second and more to the point, I'm thinking if you would only push the button, I could be halfway to my bed by now."

Moving closer to where Joan was huddling in the corner diagonally from where the elevator buttons were located, Shadow said, "The answer to your first question is that I have it on pretty good information that Christians aren't supposed to be sleeping around; that is, if you put a lot of stock in what the Holy Book says. Because if this supposed 'Christian' is doing that, then he or she would be engaging in fornication. I do believe that the Good Book says that would be a sin. And so I'd have some serious doubt about that person actually being a 'Christian.'"

Now Shadow moved close enough to Joan so she could feel his breath on her face as he finished his last sentence. She looked away, hoping to find some space to move to, but there wasn't any.

She thought, *I wish I hadn't dressed so lightly; he's bigger and stronger than me and could tear this robe and nightgown off me in no time at all.* Wanting to prevent what she just knew was about to happen, she said in a voice several registers higher, "Shadow, we're in church; you can't do this!"

"Church," Shadow said. "There's all kind of churches, Missy. And there are all kinds of people in them, too! Randy's a prime example. I don't care what he says about changing. That's all garbage! What makes you think this church is so special? Maybe it would have been special if the late bishop were still here. He was a good guy. I'll admit that, and I'm sure going to miss him. But this new dude, well, most of us know a little something about him, don't we? Even that punk kid, Vince, has the dope on him. If he was a woman he'd be called a whore, he's slept around so much. So you see, Missy, there's nothing special about this church, not now anyway."

Much to their surprise, the elevator gave off a binging sound as it arrived at the lower level. Caught up in their drama, as it were, neither one, Shadow seething with lust or Joan overwhelmed with anxiety and fear, observed the elevator's door closing or the elevator making its descent. Almost immediately, the door opened, and there stood Chandra. Her eyes were slightly red, suggesting how sleepy and tired she was, but she was smiling nevertheless.

She said, "Oh, there you are, Roomy. I wondered what had become of you. I got up to use the restroom and noticed that you were gone. I know this is a church, but from the personal things you left on your bed, one can't be too careful, if you know what I mean. So I thought, tired or not, I'd better go and look for you. Hey, Shadow, given all that you've been through, I'd have thought you'd be sleeping quite heavily about now. Okay, she who has been found, why don't we all go and get whatever sleep there is left before the sun actually does come up?"

While Chandra was speaking, Shadow was slowly moving away from Joan. When she finished, he was standing at least four feet away from her. He forced a weak smile and said, "I was coming to see you about my hand here, but Ms. Joan was kind enough to put some ice on it, that is, until I could come and have you take a look at it."

"Well, Shadow," Chandra said, "From the looks of it, I'd say she did a real fine job with your hand. Right now, however, I'd simply say, not wanting to be flip or anything, just put a few more ice cubes on it and call me in the morning—very late in the morning. Come on, Roomy, we should get some rest. See you later, Shadow."

Not looking at Shadow, Joan quickly stepped out of the elevator and began walking over to where the Chandra was standing. Holding the open door button all of this time, Shadow finally stepped out of the elevator and allowed the door to close. Watching them casually move down the hallway, he said at the top of his voice, "Good morning, ladies, and thank you again, Ms. Joan, for looking after my hand."

Without saying a word or looking back at him, Joan simply waved her left hand.

As they walked, Chandra said wearily, "He sounds so chipper at this time of the morning. What's his story, I wonder?"

"It's a short story, very short, believe me, but I'm not in a mood to talk about it now," Joan said. "By the way, I didn't leave any 'personal things' lying around, except if you call costume jewelry 'personal.'

"That's fine with me," Chandra said, "because right now, neither am I. 'Personal things', I was just messing with Shadow. The way he had you cornered, he had this look on his face like he was just about to sit down to a Thanksgiving dinner. The fool, now he knows what it's like to go hungry!"

When they were on their side of the Family Life Center and in their room, Chandra, as she had done earlier, promptly dropped onto her bed and, in no time at all, was asleep.

Joan, on the other hand, sat on her bed, staring off into the space of the partially lit room. She wondered, *What kind of mess have I gotten myself into now? What does Shadow know about Steve and me? He acts like he might know a lot, but who would have told him anything? To hear him tell it, I'm pretty much in the same boat as the new young minister here. But how can that be? We were just having a simple affair, a very private and secret one, or so I thought. What do I do now? What will people say about me . . . now?* These thoughts caused her emotions to boil over quickly, and she initially began whimpering and weeping. Then it became stronger. In an effort to muffle the sounds of her weeping, she covered her mouth with one of the pillows on the bed.

She continued sobbing for a little longer, and that gave way to whimpering. As her bloodshot eyes grew heavy, she slowly let go of the pillow that she had been holding over her mouth, allowing it to drift onto the floor. Clearly sleepy now, she eased herself from a sitting position to a curled up ball on the bed. In no time at all, she was fast asleep.

CHAPTER TWENTY-THREE

S TEVE FINALLY ARRIVED at his destination. After taking an
inquisitive look through the windows in the door of each office, he
had leisurely made his way to the small chapel. Before entering, he paused
to take in the unique, oval-shaped room with its ambience of soft lights
and scented aroma. Then he stepped inside and walked briskly down
the center aisle to the platform at the front of the chapel. He stood for
several minutes, looking up at the podium and the picture above, and
then he slowly lowered himself to his knees.

He bowed his head and said aloud, "You will forgive me if I don't
do this right, Lord, won't You? I've never . . . you know, never really
prayed . . . seriously before. Randy says that I'm a Christian now, but I
still feel like I've got to get a great deal more off of my chest, you know . . .
like asking Mia . . . well, You know, asking her to forgive me . . . for what
I did to her. If she had known what Joan and I were doing, it would have
hurt her really badly. I'd tell her it wasn't her fault, that it wasn't anything
that she did . . . or didn't do. It was all me, Lord, You know, thinking I
had it all together. But I wasn't very smart. I was just very selfish and too
full of myself to seriously consider her feelings, not to mention Joan's.

Chapter Twenty-Three

Joan is still here . . . maybe she will forgive me . . . I need to ask her to forgive me."

No sooner had he uttered these words than he recalled what he had promised himself. That is, as weak as he was, he needed to avoid being around Joan. Painfully, he admitted, "What do I do if I'm tempted again? Joan's a very attractive woman and so willing, that I may not be able to restrain myself. What will I do? What will You do with me? Maybe You should just take me out now, Lord! Why waste time with a no-good cheater . . . on my beloved wife . . . and other people who trusted me . . . like my students and teachers?"

As tears began to pour down his face, this admission of weakness forced him to cry out, "Help me, Lord! Have mercy on me! Show me how to deal with my sin-ridden self, Lord!"

Trying to regain his composure, he lifted his right arm to wipe away his tears and found himself looking up at the podium. He wasn't sure what he was seeing. He didn't recall seeing it before when he came into the chapel, but there it was—a bright light seemingly coming from the top of the podium.

He rose slowly to a standing position and began making his way up the two steps to the podium. It was only when he was standing alongside it that he became aware of how large a structure it was. He also observed that the outer edges of the podium's dark surface were stained with small water marks. Tears, he surmised. They let him know that he wasn't the only person to have visited this chapel.

He thought, *If these marks are tear stains, then maybe I can find solace here in the small chapel.*

The light he had noticed was coming from the opened Bible resting on the podium. This was indeed the Bible that Randy had told him about. Seeing it brought more tears to his eyes, and he whispered, "Thank You, Lord, thank You, thank You for answering my prayer. You heard what I was trying to pray about, but how can I be sure?"

As soon as he looked down, he saw that the Bible was opened to the book of Colossians chapter 2, verses 13 and 14. He read and seemed to hear, "When you were dead in your sins and in the uncircumcision of your sinful nature, God made you alive with Christ. He forgave us all our sins, having canceled the written code, with its regulations, that was against us and that stood opposed to us; he took it away, nailing it to the cross."

The pages appeared to turn themselves, and they came to rest at the book of First John chapter 5, verse 13. Once again, he read and heard, "I write these things to you who believe in the name of the Son of God so that you may know that you have eternal life."

Steve continued to be overwhelmed by what he was experiencing, as each new level of brightness took him to a different scripture. In response, he asked, "Thank You, Lord, but what do I do now?"

Once again, the pages turned and took him to the book of Colossians chapter 2, verses 6 and 7. He saw and heard, "So then, just as you received Christ Jesus as Lord, continue to live in him, rooted and built up in him, strengthened in the faith as you were taught, and overflowing with thankfulness."

The pages turned again, taking him to the book of Philippians chapter 2, verse 13, where he read, "For it is God who works in you to will and to act in order to fulfill his good purpose."

That level of brightness was accompanied by the pages turning further in Philippians to chapter 4, verse 6, "Do not be anxious about anything, but in every situation, by prayer and petition, with thanksgiving, present your request to God."

What followed was even brighter than the earlier presentation of Scripture. Steve saw and heard the book of John chapter 14, verse 26, "But the Counselor, the Holy Spirit, whom the Father will send in my name, will teach you all things and will remind you of everything I have said to you."

As he continued to stare at the verse he had just read, the light coming forth from the Bible began to fade. Steve interpreted this as an indication that his Bible lesson was over for the time being. He slowly stepped back from the podium with his head bowed. As he did so, he said softly, "Thank You, Lord. Thank You. Thank You. This is what I needed to understand, to know where I stood with You."

With a new sense of humility, he moved respectfully down the two steps and began walking toward the doorway.

Strolling back from the little chapel, Steve was still in a meditative state. As he approached the Family Life Center, it struck him that something was different. No need to guess about it, he was different. He was not the same man entering the Center as the one who had, hours ago, desperately stumbled out of it. How could he be the same person after his radical decision to accept Jesus Christ as his Lord and Savior? Accompanying this cognitive recognition and awareness on his part were new and rich feelings of lightness and peacefulness.

He thought, *I feel like I'm walking on air, I feel so different. Mia would be overjoyed if she knew . . . maybe she does . . . I hope she does.*

Reaching for one of the doors to the Center, he noticed the time on his watch. "Three forty-five," he whispered to himself. "I better try not to wake up the guys again as I did earlier."

So he opened the door ever so slowly and quietly. Stepping inside, he noticed that the large room wasn't as dark as it had been earlier.

This is a good sign, he thought. *I won't be tripping over C. J.'s stuff and waking him up again. Although, if he did wake up, it would be nice to share with him what has happened to me. I'm sure he'd be much more interested than Shadow was.*

He tiptoed over to his cot and lowered himself gently onto it. "I feel like I could sleep for days now," he whispered to no one in particular while allowing his eyes to close.

CHAPTER TWENTY-FOUR

AFTER TOSSING AND turning several times, Joan finally sat up.
Her little clock on the dresser read three forty-seven. As she looked
around, trying to make sense of where she was, it slowly came back to
her when she spotted the person lying on the other bed across the room.

*From the way she's clutching that black bag, it has to be Dr. Wilson-
Ross. Thank goodness, it's her!* She thought. *And of course, we're at Saint
Augustine Baptist Church's Family Life Center. So far, so good; but what
woke me up? Why am I feeling so clammy? What was I dreaming? Oh, my,
I was dreaming about being in a place where I couldn't escape! Where was
it? Was it here in the church or somewhere else? It had to be here—the dream
seemed so real and so horrible. I'm remembering eyes, yes, eyes looking down
at me. And there were also voices shouting names at me! Names, terrible
names like hypocrite! Whore! Cheap slut! Heavens, how could I have had a
dream like that in church of all places?'*

Then as if she were hit by a lightning bolt, it came to her. *Shadow,
that terrible, nasty man! Shadow! He's to blame for all of this! He was so nice
when we first met; now he's just an evil man trying to hurt me. He thinks
that he knows all about me. And if he goes around telling what he thinks
he does know, I'd be ruined. No one will ever respect me again.*

Chapter Twenty-Four

Clutching her waist with her left hand and covering her mouth with her right, as if to brace herself against the rejection she anticipated would follow Shadow snitching on her, she thought, *My church member, Mother Loving, who came here with me, Sister Agnes, and the other women won't want to have anything to do with me! For that matter, I'll become an outcast, and all of the other folks here will avoid me too! What can I do?*

She was unable to quell these painful thoughts, and her eyes once again began to fill with tears that rushed down both sides of her face. Almost weirdly, she simultaneously felt a sharp pain in her lower abdomen. With this change of focus, she stopped crying as quickly as she had started. The reason, her body was telling her that she had been holding herself in the same position for an unusual period of time, and she'd better do something about it now! Not wanting the pain to intensify, she threw her legs over the side of her bed, thrust her feet into her tennis shoes, snatched up her robe, and was off to the bathroom!

Joan quickly removed the chain, hurriedly opened the suite door, and dashed down the hall to bathroom where the signage above the door read "WOMEN." Hurriedly, she pushed the door open, almost knocking down Sister Agnes. Surprised, Joan said, "Oh, I'm so sorry. I didn't mean to hurt you. Are you okay? I don't know why I always wait so long and then I have to rush like a crazy person. I'm so sorry, Sister Agnes."

Sister Agnes, initially stunned by the near collision, took a few minutes to gather herself. Then she said, "Don't worry about me, child, go ahead and take care of yourself. I'll be okay once I catch my breath. Well, you take care. See you later."

Sister Agnes paused for a moment in front of the door before attempting to exit, lest some other foolish person come rushing through and take her out for sure. As she was about to open the door, she heard, "Sister Agnes, I know it's late, early, or something, but could you wait for me? I desperately need to ask you something?"

A little taken aback by the impromptu but urgent-sounding request, Sister Agnes frowned and then, chuckling, said, "Well, sure, child, I'll be just outside the door. But hurry if you can— I'm accustomed to getting at least eight hours of sleep a night." Pulling the door open and going outside to wait for Joan, she heard her say, "Thank you ever so much, Sister Agnes. You don't know what this means to me."

Several minutes later, Joan appeared, smiling and rubbing her hands together. She said, "That's a bathroom to die for; there's everything a woman would want, except for the bidet. Even this lotion smells so nice and feels luxurious."

Smiling back, Sister Agnes said, "The late bishop thought of everything, with the help of the Women's Auxiliary Union. I can't speak for the men's facilities, of course, but ours turned out quite nicely, I must say. Well now, enough of that. *What* is it that you 'so desperately' need to talk about at this hour of the morning?"

Looking around as if she wasn't very comfortable about sharing in the hallway, Joan initially said, "Well," she paused and then continued, "I wish I could invite you to my suite, but I don't want to wake my roommate, the good Dr. Wilson-Ross. She has had some night, I tell you."

"Well then, surely we want her to rest. We're putting a lot on her," Sister Agnes said. "We can go to my suite. We won't be disturbing anyone there. I'm just three doors down, child."

Joan, smiling, said, "You have your own suite. I'm impressed."

"Oh, it's no biggie; it was a small token from my late husband, for whom the Center is named, you know. Come, child—it's late."

With Sister Agnes leading the way, they hurried down to her suite.

When they arrived at the suite, Sister Agnes's fingers flew rapidly over the keys of a small control panel outside the suite's door. The door opened and slid into the right side of the wall. Smiling at Joan, she said, "He was forever concerned about my safety, thinking that a door requiring a combination would help that. However, having to open and close the door this way can be a real nuisance every time you go out and come in. But do come in, won't you?"

Chapter Twenty-Four

Once they were inside, Sister Agnes repeated what she had done a few seconds ago, only this time to the small key pad located on the left side of the doorway. The door immediately began to close.

"That's very gracious of you, Sister Agnes. I know I'm really imposing on your rest and time. I want you to know that I deeply appreciate your willingness to meet with me. Now I don't know quite where to start," Joan said.

"Oh, child," Sister Agnes said, "start anywhere, but I think we'll find the parlor a little more comfortable. This way, please."

Sister Agnes led Joan into the parlor through an ample vestibule decorated with pictures of her late husband and herself when they were much younger, as well as pictures of other relatives. As Joan stepped into the room, she placed her hand over her mouth. Sister Agnes's parlor was no ordinary parlor. It was decorated very much along the lines that one sees in an exquisite magazine. A large, leather, cordovan-colored couch, two handsome chairs in a floral pattern of purple, teal, and light tan, a huge rug with a border with the same colors, and a good-sized, cherry coffee table with several objects de art on it filled this room.

Joan, quite overcome at what she was seeing, plopped down into one of the two larger chairs. Sister Agnes sat down on the leather couch directly across from her, smiling, and said, "Well, child, what is it that can't wait until morning?"

CHAPTER TWENTY-FIVE

JOAN SMILED BACK and, letting her head slowly drift downward so that she was looking directly at the rug, said softly, "I'm a thirty-five year old black woman, a teacher, with few prospects of getting a man, and I fell in love with a married man. A married man who apparently lost his wife in all this mess we're dealing with right now. I know this sounds so cliché. I know that I should have known better than that; clearly I should have known better. I'm really a faithful church member as well as the church secretary . . . I'm supposed to be a Christian… does that surprise you?

"If this is the case, you may be wondering what's really worrying me, why I can't sleep tonight, this morning, or whatever time it is. I'll tell you. I'm worried that one of the individuals who came to this very church, this sanctuary, like the rest of us, may have found out about my ridiculous affair and will tell all. When he does so, I don't know what to do, Sister Agnes. I don't know what to do about it."

Sister Agnes sat pensively as she listened to Joan pour out her heart. She thought, *Isn't it interesting how God has a way of retuning you to life's lessons that you have experienced in the past? I guess the reasons must be first, to keep you humble and second, to have you share how God's grace was visited upon you time and again and again and again.* She listened but said nothing for a space of five minutes.

All the while sitting there in the quiet, Joan found herself becoming a bit anxious as she waited for Sister Agnes to respond to her little pitiful and shameful tale. *Have I said too much?* she wondered, *or been too forthcoming to this complete stranger?*

Maybe the miracle she was expecting wasn't going to happen in this parlor, at this time, and with this person.

Just then, she heard Sister Agnes' voice saying something to the effect, "That was quite a mouthful to be getting out at this time of the morning." It snapped Joan back from her painful reflections, and she looked up to meet Sister Agnes's gaze head-on. Sister Agnes seemed neither alarmed nor disappointed and not even surprised. Instead, what Joan encountered were soft eyes, a gentle smile, and a sense of understanding.

Sister Agnes said softly, "I can only think that sharing what you did had to be extremely hard for you. I am deeply humbled that you chose me, child."

"It had to be you. You know, just the way you carry yourself, you're so spiritual. And I couldn't go to the new, little minister, not at this time of the morning and not with this tale of woe," Joan said with pleading in her voice.

"You are most kind," Sister Agnes said. "But you can only know a book when you have read all of it; for the cover can often be either confusing or misleading. I have but two things, maybe three, to say to you before rushing you off to whatever sleep is left this morning. First, wherever you are in your walk with God, it's important to know that He is a God of many, many chances. If it were not so, I don't believe you and I would be having this conversation. His Son has already taken home those who showed their consistent love for Him. He doesn't need to fool with any of us except as a loving God, a merciful God, and, thank goodness, a forgiving God. He is not willing for any of us to miss what He has planned for us.

We Have Not Been Listening: The Awakening

"Second, I don't believe it's by accident that you and I are speaking about this situation that's confronting you. I truly believe it's a part of God's plan for you to get your life back on track and for *me* to remember how loving, how gracious, and how merciful He is to us all. Child, I've been where you are, and God did not throw me under the bus, as it were! Instead, He reached out to me, loved me, forgave me, and provided a path for me to walk on if I wanted to do so. You have to understand that your crisis didn't just start a few hours ago; it began the moment Jesus the Christ took home all those who chose to believe He saved and redeemed them from their sins. From that point on, those of us who were not taken were left in a major state of crisis!"

CHAPTER TWENTY-SIX

"NOW I SAID that I only had two things for you, but come to think of it, I actually have a third thing for you. I'm not sure what your feelings are about it, but I can remember confusing sex for love and confusing intimacy for the short-term fireworks that accompanied it. And when the physical release was all over, the only feelings left were shame and guilt. I truly believe that's what David, the king of Israel in the Old Testament, must have felt after his terrible affair with Bathsheba, especially when he learned that God also knew. But in the fifty-first Psalm, he pled for God's forgiveness and repented of his sins. God heard his prayers and forgave him! What was available for David back then is available to you even now! All you need to do is ask Him, and He will quickly grant it.

"Now here's the important part of what I'm telling you, child. The mess that you got yourself into isn't going to simply disappear, as if it never happened, once you take God up on His promise. You will, just like David, have to deal with the turmoil that follows what you've created; but God did not simply leave him hanging. He was with David as he moved through the challenges that followed. Once David accepted God's forgiveness for his sins, he, David, did not have to feel guilty or shameful after that. Satan could try, really only attempt, to accuse him of his terrible adultery and murder, but David was forgiven by God. His sins were put away 'as far as the east is from the west.'

Child, the same gift God gave David is available to you now, this very minute. This is also your comeback to anyone attempting to accuse you of any former sin! We don't have a minute to waste! What do you say?"

"Sister Agnes," Joan said, "I can't say that I've ever heard the Word put the way you just did. It was most definitely heartfelt. It tells me that I have missed being someone who sought to live the Word, not only talk about it. I want what you have or seem to have; it's desirable and attractive. Most of all, it's genuine. What do I have to do?"

"Pray with me silently, child, as I do so aloud," Sister Agnes said. She began, 'Lord God, most holy, I come to understand that I'm nothing without You. I also come to know that all my righteousness is as fifty rags! I thought that I had settled my relationship with You sometime before, but quite obviously I hadn't. I thought being a church member was sufficient, but it isn't. I thought working in the church made me right for heaven, but it hasn't made me worthy of very much. I know now that I need You in my life if I'm to take advantage of Your many, many blessings. I hereby confess my sins and deeply ask for your forgiveness, Lord. Amen.'

"Now lest I appear rude, child, let's get you off to bed, and we can talk more at a later time. Okay?"

"Yes, sure," Joan said, "thank you ever so much for all you have done for me. I knew you were the right person, I just knew it!" She stood up as Sister Agnes was also standing. Joan took a few steps toward Sister Agnes and embraced her.

Sister Agnes said jokingly, "Child, if you crush my bones, I won't be around to know how grateful you are. Just remember that God, God is good all the time! Now off to bed with you."

And with that she withdrew from Joan's embrace.

CHAPTER TWENTY-SEVEN

I N THE DEAD of winter, as cold as it had been, it wasn't usual for
the sun to be out; needless to say, for it to be so bright and as strong
as it was this morning. But as the saying goes, "If you don't like the
weather, just wait a minute or so, and it will change."

Whatever the reason for the sun's fullness and richness, Carlos was
receiving quite an ample dose of it, since he hadn't moved from the desk
chair he had occupied earlier. In fact, he was positioned right in front
of the west wing window with the purple and gold curtains opened and
the sun was pouring directly down on him.

Notwithstanding his inability to see, the combined strength of the
sun's brilliance and warmth was sufficient to stir him. Initially rubbing
his eyes, but also partially shielding them, he whispered, "This is quite a
'wake-up call,' Lord, even for a blind man. I've always thought You had
a sense of humor. In my case, a trumpet, You know, one of those alto
trumpets would have done quite well. I think I still have my hearing, or
at least the last time I raised my voice, it seemed I had it. But I'm still
listening, Lord. Good morning, Lord."

He paused for a few seconds and continued, "To be perfectly honest, Lord, if I sound a little sarcastic it's just that this thing with the sun is a very clear reminder that I can't see! I can't see!"

His eyes began to glisten with a trace of moisture. "I know I've messed up royally; I know that I was just going through the motions, playing church and all, but for what You want me to do . . . how in the world am I going to be able to do anything . . . if I can't see!" Just then, tears came gushing forth from his eyes, flooding down his face.

While using his hands to wipe away the tears that had spilled over, Carlos began to sense an eerie stillness that he had experienced before. The room also felt darker as the light began to disappear. More stillness, then a gentle voice saying, "Move away from the desk."

Carlos stood up, pushed the desk chair away from him, and slowly began making his way to the right of the desk. No sooner had he done so than there was a roaring sound that became louder and louder. A sound of this sort is typically associated with tornadoes. Not only was the sound overwhelming, but he was feeling caught up, as it were, amidst twirling winds.

Not sure what was happening to him, Carlos blurted, "God, I'm sorry. I didn't mean all of that." The next thing he knew for certain was that he was on his hands and knees, resting on carpet again.

"Lord, where am I?" he asked.

"You are where I found you when you decided to return to me."

"I remember now. I was kneeling in the middle of the bishop's office, and I was trying to tell You that I wasn't Your guy; that I wasn't the man for the job. But You didn't listen . . . and You took my sight. Are You now planning to fire me and give me back my sight?"

"No. That is not why I brought you back to where you began. You were brought back to go forward again. You were brought back to know My love, to know My mercy, and to know My grace for you. Most important of all, you were brought back, to know for certain, as I told Joshua, that what I want you to do, I WILL DO IT!

Chapter Twenty-Seven

"As I was with Moses, Joshua, and Solomon, so I will be with you. Now the time is short. Go and have the young sister ready for the work she needs to do."

"Lord, I'm speechless . . . because I know You care for and love me; who else would do that for a pig-headed creep like me . . . and I thank You for staying with me and not giving up on me. And I also thank You for saving Sister Minister. She should be, as I've tried to say, standing here right now. But Your will be done, Lord; Your will be done. Thank You again, Lord, for this day and how You love . . . even me. Now I best get a move on."

CHAPTER TWENTY-EIGHT

Bsomething coming UT AS CARLOS attempted to move, it struck him that the whole
time God had been speaking with him, he had been kneeling. As he
positioned himself to stand, his balance was a little wobbly. After a few
fumbling attempts, he finally stood, but now he had another challenge; he
was uncertain which direction to take. He very cautiously turned around
in a circular fashion and said, "I know this study like the back of my hand,
but not standing in the middle of it, blind. Without some way to see, I
don't know east from west or north from south. I'm not complaining,
Lord, but the truth is the truth, and . . . and it's not setting me free . . . yet."

He had no sooner finished speaking when he felt something coming
back to him. "Hmm, what's this?" he said and spoke a little louder. "Tell
me something, Lord. Can I move from here?"

This question resulted in something coming back to him a second
time. His voice raised even louder now, he said, "Okay, so the mirror the
bishop used to make sure he looked okay before leaving his office is facing
me. That means his bathroom is facing in the opposite direction! And I'm
sure my nose will tell me if I'm close. Yes, that's it. His special cologne
that he liked so much will tell me if I'm close. I don't know if You're
laughing all over heaven, Lord, but thanks for the other four senses."

Chapter Twenty-Eight

As Carlos was about to enter the small hallway leading to the bishop's bathroom, he heard a knock on the bishop's study door. "Here we go again," Carlos said aloud. "Just when I thought I was in control of my life, I'm completely helpless. By the time I get to the door, if I don't kill myself, it will probably be the spring of next year."

He decided to simply call out, "Can I help you?

He heard, "It's C. J., and I have the clothing you wanted me to pick up for you."

Carlos replied, "C. J., on the key chain that I gave you the other day, there is a unique key with a small 'B' on it. When you have located it, use it to open the study door. Thanks for your help."

A few minutes passed before Carlos heard the sound of a key working its way into the lock on the study door. Then the door opened and C. J. stepped inside. He said, "Good morning, sir— oh, sorry, Reverend. I hope you slept well. Where do you want me put your clothing?"

"Right this way. There are some hooks in the bishop's bathroom. Put them on the hooks, okay? So how are you doing this morning after your experience last night, C. J.?"

"Well, to tell you the truth, I'm still a little sleepy but not so much from the deal with Vince. After that was over, I was too hyped up to go right back to the Center and go to sleep. So I made my way down the hallway and ended up at the small chapel.

"You know, the thing you said about needing to have a special relationship with our Lord, well, that really hit me. And I took the opportunity in that special place to really establish what I hope will be a great relationship with Him. Earlier in the evening I was thinking maybe I was too late; but He kept the door open for me, Reverend, for even me."

"Hey, man, C. J., I'm so pleased to hear that. God is a God of endless chances, if we only give Him a chance to share His forgiveness and love! Hallelujah! God be praised! This is the kind of news I'd like to get every morning. This is great, C. J."

"Well, sir, that's just one of the reasons I'm a little sleepy, an important one to be sure. But after I left the small chapel, excited about my commitment to Jesus Christ, I immediately ran into my first faith challenge in the person of Shadow. He's a grown man, possibly in his late thirties, early forties, a little unpolished, but an adult, supposedly. Now I know that I have to pray for him, but the man acted so childish, so help me! I barely know the guy, and I don't know what I did to him. But somehow, he is angry at me for trying to help out here. I've turned him over to God as I've said, but the way he acted sure messed with me at the time. I just hope I won't have these challenges too often.

"After that, when I finally got to the Center and was in my bed, feeling I could at least catch a nap, that's when Steve, you know the big, tall guy who's a high school principal, started having some kind of panic attack. In his haste to get out of the Center, he woke a few of us up, quite noisily, I might add. Randy and the older deacon were among some of the guys whose sleep was interrupted. Randy asked me to get the doctor since we didn't know initially what was wrong with Steve. So it has been quite a night/morning, sir."

"I can see that, pardon the pun; and then you had to get up early to bring me my clothing. This has been quite a morning for you, C. J.; not uneventful by any stretch of the imagination. I deeply appreciate you getting my things and thanks for sharing, C. J.

"You undoubtedly know this, C. J., but as a way of keeping us on our toes, bear with me, okay?"

"Certainly, sir," C. J. said.

"The enemy hasn't been sleeping, now has he?" Carlos asked rhetorically. "We have to figure that it was just a matter of time before he would be getting busy after us. We also have to remember that he had written us off, but now he got some mo' of God's chillun to deal with! And he doesn't plan to make it any easier on us than he did on those who went before us, I promise you that. So please don't feel that you have been singled out, C. J., because of the fantastic decision you made this morning. Testing is just a part of what we have signed on to. By the way, what is the hour, C. J.?"

"It's eight on the head, sir," C. J. said.

Chapter Twenty-Eight

"Okay, about the time . . . when we finished up after our late night service, I had hoped to get an earlier start on our day, but given all that has happened in the meantime, it's probably more realistic to start the day off around noon. That should give folks ample time to get ready for the remainder of the day. Sound good?"

"That's fine with me, sir," C. J. said, "but I'm not too sure, after sleeping in my clothes all night, what even a little water will do for me!"

"Well, son, for the answer to your concerns, you have come to the right church. Saint Augustine, I'll have you know, was voted for the past five years the most civic-minded Protestant church in our community. What this means is that over the years, we have gathered lots of clothing as well as foodstuff to be given away to the needy. The clothing, in particular, is not just some discarded items that folks got tired of or outgrew. I'd say about eighty-five percent of the clothing that was given to the church was brand new. And some of the clothing even has designers' labels on it. So you have come to the right place, my young friend. I'd check with Randy, and he'll be able to put you in fresh, new clothing so that our soap and water doesn't go to waste. Sound like a winner, C. J.?"

"Sure does," C. J. said. "That news really lifts my spirits because if the church didn't have the resources, I would feel very uncomfortable wearing the same clothing over and over again. Okay, I'll be on my way so I can get cleaned up."

"One quick thing before you get going, C. J.," Carlos said. "Remember when you used the tape recorder the other night? Okay, at the same location there are several CDs; actually there's one for each book of the Bible. Find the one for the book of Joshua and put that one into the CD player, okay? Be sure to turn it up a bit so I can hear it over the shower. Thanks again for all of your help. Come back for me after you have gotten all cleaned up."

"No problem, sir. I'll put your disc in and then be off," C. J. said.

Carlos turned and headed toward the bishop's bathroom, and as he reached the bathroom door, he paused to hear the beginning of the book of Joshua on the CD:

We Have Not Been Listening: The Awakening

Now after the death of Moses the servant of the Lord it came to pass that the Lord spake unto Joshua the son of Nun, Moses' minister, saying, Moses my servant is dead; now therefore arise, go over Jordan, thus and all this people, unto the land which I do give to them, even to the children of Israel.

Then he heard the door to the bishop's study close and figured that C. J. had waited to make sure the CD player was working before leaving. He resumed listening and heard:

There shall not any man be able to stand before thee all the days of thy life: as I was with Moses, so I will be with thee: I will not fail thee, nor forsake thee. Be strong and of a good courage: for unto this people thou shall divide for an inheritance the land, which I sware unto their fathers to give them. Only be thou strong and very courageous, that thou mayest observe to do according to all the law, which Moses my servant commanded thee: turn not from it to the right hand or to the left, that thou mayest prosper whithersoever thou goest.

This book of the law shall not depart out of thy mouth; but thou shalt meditate therein day and night, that thou mayest observe to do according to all that is written therein; for then thou make thy way prosperous, and then thou shalt have good success. Have I not commanded thee? Be strong and of a good courage; be not afraid, neither be thou dismayed: for the Lord thy God is with thee whithersoever thou goest.

Carlos shook his head and said aloud, "Hmm, **'Be strong and of a good courage'** was stated at least three times! Man, given the level of responsibility that Joshua was about to assume, he was definitely in need of some heavy encouragement. So I guess I'm in good company with my pitiful self." With that he moved into the bishop's bathroom.

CHAPTER TWENTY-NINE

ONCE HE HAD showered and was fully attired, Carlos began clapping his hands loudly as another way of creating sound waves which would come back at him. In so doing, it let him know when he was approaching a wall or some solid object, like a desk or even a chair. This method proved quite effective for him, because it allowed him to avoid bumping into anything that could hurt him. In fact, this method allowed him to cross the bishop's large office to come within a few feet of the front door of the office. When he stopped walking, Carlos bowed his head and said, "I know that just clapping my hands as a means of avoiding things isn't really what's allowing me to move around. I thank You that You have allowed the Holy Spirit to be my actual guide. As You were with Joshua, so You are with me. Thank you, Lord."

As he approached the door, he heard a knock and a voice saying, "Sir it's C. J. I'm back."

"Great timing C. J., I'm ready to go. Use the key again, and we can be on our way," Carlos said.

He heard the tumblers moving in the lock, and the door to the bishop's office opened. Carlos felt the slightly warm air from the hallway, and he took a few steps out into it.

We Have Not Been Listening: The Awakening

He was greeted with, "Good morning again, sir. Boy, does it feel good to be clean, I'm telling you."

"So Randy was able to hook you up with some fresh clothing?" Carlos asked.

"He sure did; you guys, I mean the church, has an actual 'big box store' in the Family Life Center. I mean it's something I wouldn't expect to be a part of a church," C. J. said.

"The Bishop was very community-oriented and felt the church should be ready to meet as many of the needs the community might have as possible. He always used to say, 'Be you ever-so-ready, for you know not when you will be left on your own.'"

"That's quite prophetic, wouldn't you say? So then he must have been prepared for the Lord taking home of His own?" C. J. asked.

"I'd like to think he was," Carlos said, "but given all that has taken place over the last twelve hours or so, and this is painful to say, I'm inclined to believe he was neither prepared nor preparing for the Lord's taking home His own."

"Wow! Man!" C. J. exclaimed. "That's a heavy thing to say. I mean, he was a bishop! How could he not be up on all things related to Christ's coming for His own? How was it even possible for him not to know these things? It's just mind-boggling to think he didn't have a clue!"

"Well, C. J." Carlos said, "as you know, 'No man knowest the hour nor the day;' but given your familiarity with the Bible, you're undoubtedly aware that there were many religious leaders who were present at the time when Jesus walked the earth. None of them knew who He was, and thus they missed out on His first coming! In much the same way, sad to say, our bishop, my mentor in some respects, was a modern day religious leader who neither knew Jesus Christ as the Son of the living God nor had any understanding about His taking home those folks who clearly believed in Him."

"Somehow, Reverend," C. J. replied, "that still doesn't tell me how someone who becomes a bishop, not an ordinary preacher or whatever, could not know about the plan of salvation that God arranged for us through His Son, Jesus. I mean, how does one attend seminary, pastor several churches, preach a million sermons, and rise through the ranks to become a bishop, and still be left out of the loop? Somehow, as the saying goes, that dog won't hunt!"

"Well, C. J.," Carlos said, smiling, "sounds like the hot water and clean clothing have really got you going this morning, I must say. But consider this for a moment: if your perspective on the Bible is that it is a book wonderfully written, filled with captivating literature, where poetic license is taken every now and then, and that the central character, Jesus, simply represents a very positive ideal designed to inspire good deeds, then it would be possible. It would be possible to answer the questions that you have raised.

"You know, it's not too surprising when you think about where those of us—me, you, Randy, and some of the others—were quite recently, that is, before we decided to enter into a relationship with Jesus the Christ, even at this very late hour. So you can see that it's not very difficult to be in the 'house of God' but not have God resting within *your* house that is within your heart.

"In a nutshell, our bishop understood the Bible to be about doing good works primarily. He bought the social gospel lock, stock, and barrel. With that in mind, he followed Jesus, as you would follow any inspirational leader, but not as his Redeemer, Savior, and Lord. Make any sense?"

"Yes, it does. Thank you, Reverend. It's just so sad. I mean, to acquire all that education and become such an influential figure and then miss out because you couldn't believe that Jesus is Who He says He is. Man! Well, here we are at the elevator, sir," C. J. said.

"Good," Carlos said, "let's get down to the infirmary."

"Are we going to check on Vince, sir?" C. J. asked.

"We'll look in on him for sure," Carlos said with a chuckle, "but we have to see about someone else."

CHAPTER THIRTY

JUST BEFORE THEY reached the Jensen Family Life Center, Carlos said, "C. J., I need for you to have Sister Agnes and Randy meet me in the infirmary. After you have done so, wait for me here, okay?"

"Certainly," C. J. said. "Do you want me to escort you to the infirmary first?'

"Splendid idea, my young friend, splendid idea," Carlos said with a chuckle.

They walked in silence until they reached the entrance to the infirmary. C. J. spoke first, "Here we are, sir, at the infirmary. Do you want to wait out front after I bring the others, or . . . ?"

"Why don't we go inside?" Carlos said, "and once you have set me in front of the bay where Sister Minister is resting, then you can go and bring the others, okay? Now as I recall, her bay is the one located on the far right hand side."

"By all means, sir," C. J. replied.

"C. J.," Carlos said, smiling, "I thought we had an understanding."

"Understanding sir?" C. J. said. "I'm not sure I follow what you mean."

"The 'understanding' that I'm referring to, C. J., was that you were to drop the 'sir' bit," Carlos said.

Chapter Thirty

"Oh, yes, sir . . . ," C. J. said. "I guess that it seems the right thing to do . . . and it's kind of a hard habit to break . . . uh, sir. But I will work on doing so, um, Reverend. Here you are, Reverend, just as you asked, in front of the bay where Sister Minister is resting. If you don't mind, sir—see what I mean—anyway, I'd very much like to know how it is that you call this lady 'Sister Minister.'"

"Yes, of course, C. J.," Carlos said. "We will do that after you attend to your errand. See you in a little while, okay?"

"I'm on my way, sir. Oops. Sorry, Reverend," C. J. said. Embarrassed, he quickly turned and began making his way toward the door.

Upon hearing the door close behind C. J., Carlos lowered himself to the gray concrete floor and raising his arms upward, said, "As You have asked dear Lord, here I am. What would You have me to do?"

As soon as Carlos had spoken these words, the area around him grew brighter. Although he could not see the visible change, his other senses were working just fine. That is, he immediately noticed the most delightful aroma of myrrh, sweet cinnamon, calamus, cassia, and olive oil, felt a familiar presence, and heard, "Take off your shoes, for the ground you are standing upon is holy ground. Pray and wait, for you are to be an instrument of My mercy this day. And for those who are to come, they will be a witness, that as I was with Joshua, I AM also with you!"

"Yes, Lord," Carlos whispered and hastily removed his black loafers. "You mentioned 'those who are to come.' I'm guessing that You knew already that I thought to invite the most seasoned of those present at the Saint Augustine Baptist Church. I hope I didn't overstep my bounds, Lord. I guess I will find out, eh?"

CHAPTER THIRTY-ONE

CARLOS HADN'T SETTLED very long into his meditation before it was broken by the sounds of the infirmary doors opening and the voices of Randy and Sister Agnes. Once inside, however, they immediately grew silent and abruptly stopped walking. Standing there, they were initially dumbfounded by the brilliance that surrounded Carlos. It took a few minutes before they recovered themselves, but then they nodded at each other, acknowledging that something unique was taking place in the infirmary; and because of that, they continued to remain very still.

Hearing nothing, Carlos wondered whether Randy and Sister Agnes had either been struck down dead or were possibly caught up in the moment. He said to himself, "I think the Lord would've told me if He did not want them here, too." Without further hesitation, he said quietly, "Thank you both for coming. Please take off your shoes and then come help me to my feet."

Randy and Sister Agnes gave one another a brief smile and then, holding on to the other's shoulder, slipped the right shoe off first and then the left one. Once they had completed this task, they moved forward to where Carlos was kneeling. When Carlos felt that they had both of his arms, he joined the lifting process until he was fully on his feet.

He said, "Thank you for the helping hand. Now Sister Agnes, if you would go beyond the curtain and make certain everything is as it should be and, most importantly, that our dear Sister Minister is yet with us. When you have done so, pull the curtain back and walk around to the side that allows you to see the piece of glass extruding from Sister Minister's temple. Then wait for Randy and me to come to where you are standing. Thank you."

Leaving Carlos's side, Sister Agnes did as she was instructed. Taking about five steps, she moved to the bay where Sister Minister was resting and pulled back the curtain enough to allow her to slip behind it. Returning the curtain back to its original place, she turned to see about her patient. Standing directly in front of the bed in which Sister Minister was resting, she flashed back to when C. J. had informed her that her presence was requested in the infirmary. While she was pleased to be asked, she was also glad that she had thought to come prepared, that is, carrying her nurse's little gray medical bag.

Resting the bag at the foot of the hospital bed, she looked down at the small-framed, freckled-faced woman with rust-colored braids, resting under a light blue sheet and deep blue woolen blanket, and quietly said, "Sister, if you ever come out of this mess, it's probably going to shock you! Like me, you just knew for sure you were ready, now only to discover that you were not and thus you're still here. All I can say, my dear Sister Minister, is that you've got to know that the Lord has kept you here all this time because He still has something mighty special for you to do."

She opened her bag, removed her stethoscope, and proceeded to check her patient's heart rate, breathing, and other salient vitals. When she had completed her brief examination of Sister Minister, she promptly moved to the bay's opening and pulled back the curtain and then took her place where the piece of glass was protruding from Sister Minister's left temple. She waited.

We Have Not Been Listening: The Awakening

Standing alongside Carlos, Randy thought he should say something, but nothing that seemed appropriate came to mind. However, what did come to his mind were hard and biting questions. Questions like: "This is a holy place. What's someone with your nasty background doing here? Did you forget your place? You're no minister, apostle, or one of those special people God uses sometimes. Shouldn't you just run out of here, leave the infirmary, run out of the church, and get as far away from Saint Augustine Baptist Church as you possibly can?"

As these questions took bigger bites mentally, he experienced a number of physical reactions: pulsating temples, blurred vision, sweaty palms, and a flood of perspiration rushing down his back. He was just about to cry out for help when he heard Sister Agnes pull back the curtain and Carlos say, "I need to take your elbow, Randy."

As he extended his elbow to Carlos's waiting hand, Randy said, "I don't care what you think or say, God tells me that He loves me anyhow!"

Carlos said, "You bet He does. Is there any reason to doubt? Come! There is a major blessing awaiting us in there."

As they moved forward, Randy wasn't sure how or why, but the disturbing feelings he was experiencing a few minutes before just disappeared. Perhaps it was because of the light coming from the bay that seemed even brighter than he had noticed earlier. In fact, it was so bright that he placed his left hand below his eyebrows to partially shield his eyes. When he and Carlos arrived at the bay, they promptly stopped just inside its opening.

Carlos said to Randy, "Pull the curtain behind us, for the Lord will do a wonder this day." When he heard that the curtain had been returned to its original place, Carlos said, "Let us draw nearer and take hold of each other's hands. As I pray, place your free hand upon Sister Minister's head."

He paused for a minute or two to feel certain that everything was as it should be, and then he began to pray, "Lord, I thank You for extending your grace to us, even though You know us. I thank You for loving us through the lens of the cross. Now I plead for Your continued

98

forgiveness and mercy on the three of us gathered here, for we are but ants in your sight; but You have made it possible for us to bear witness to Your miraculous power. Now merciful Father, the God of heaven and earth, glorify Yourself this day, and in so doing, grant your daughter lying here with a full measure of health to be able to serve You. It is in your blessed Son's name, Jesus, the name that is above all names, that I offer this humble prayer. Amen."

When Carlos finished praying, he paused for another few minutes or so, and then said, "Sister Agnes, take my hand that you are holding and place it right above where the glass is protruding." Hesitantly, Sister Agnes took his hand and placed it where she was instructed. But as soon as she did so, she promptly whispered, "Carlos, are you sure? . . . You could leave her paralyzed for life, ruin her speech, and do who knows what? Are you sure?"

Responding in a very calm voice, Carlos said, "This is not about me, Sister Agnes; I'm just following orders. I'm just the instrument here and nothing more. This matter is totally in God's hands, as it was before, as it is now, and as it will be in the future."

Feeling his hand touching both Sister Minister's temple and the protruding glass, he began to pray again, saying, "It is because of who You are that this glass is removed from Your darling daughter! In Jesus' name, be it removed!"

With those words, Carlos swiftly pulled the piece of glass out of Sister Minister's left temple.

CHAPTER THIRTY-TWO

WHEN C. J. returned to the men's side at the Jensen Family life Center, it was essentially empty except for a few stragglers who found it difficult to get up this morning. Not wishing to disturb them, he walked quietly and slowly to his bed. When he reached it, he just dropped down on the side facing the set of double doors. Sitting there hunched over, head down, and swiping his hands in a washing motion, C. J. was clearly dejected. In a sad, quiet voice, he asked, "Did I talk too much, complain too loudly, and speak too poorly of folks? I mean, I was up earlier than anybody else getting his things, bringing them to him, and taking him to the infirmary. Then without any justification, he just dismisses me like I hadn't done anything at all! Maybe, just maybe, I have put this brother on too high a pedestal and I need to take him off of it! And I need to do that right now!"

C. J. was just putting a final exclamation mark on his last comment when he heard, "Hey, C. J., just the man I'm looking for. Oh, sorry man, sorry. I didn't mean to catch you praying. I'm really sorry."

It was Steve, sounding as cheery as if he had just won the lottery. His words and the jubilant tone in which they were offered struck C. J. as if he were hit with an upper-cut. His head bolted upright, his chin jolted forward, and his shoulders were pushed backward. In response, he sputtered, "Uh, no, um, well, uh . . . Hey, Steve, . . . good morning to you, too."

"That's right, good morning C. J. I . . . uh . . . I need to apologize for my behavior last night or this morning, C. J. I was terribly out of line and um, I now know better. I mean, I really know better. It's amazing the kind of change that God can make in your life, I'm telling you. Look, once again, if I interrupted your quiet time, man, I'm sorry. I know you have a Bible, and I was just wondering if I might borrow it for a brief spell . . . and have a little quiet time myself. Mia, my wife, used to do that . . . you know, have some time with the Lord, and I would just laugh at her. What a fool I was. Sorry, too much information. But if I can borrow it, I will bring it back to you before lunch."

All the while Steve was sharing his upbeat mood, C. J., on the other hand, began feeling shameful and guilty. He said to himself, *Fool! Here I'm learning that Steve must have found the Lord sometime early this morning, and he's trying to tell me about it in an indirect way, and I'm caught up in my own self-pitying funk. Well, Lord, if You can, please, please forgive me! The enemy is so slick! He wants me to focus on me and how I'm feeling about no longer being the go-to guy for the new minister. I just need to remember that whatever I'm doing, it is not for anyone else but You, Lord!*

Reaching for his Bible, he said, "Why, of course you can borrow it, Steve. But what are you telling me, guy?"

Laughing, Steve said, "C. J., I thought you'd never ask. But being serious for a minute, I'm glad that I'm having a chance to tell someone who might care. I mean, Shadow didn't have a clue what I was talking about when I told him that I had accepted Jesus Christ as my Lord and Savior. You at least are familiar with these things since your father's a minister and you were raised in the church. So at the very least, you would know where I'm coming from."

"Wow! Glory to God! Awesome! Awesome, my brother! What else can I say, Steve? Wow! I'm really glad to get the 'good news,' Steve!

"This is just the pick-me-up I needed. God can do some mighty heavy things for us, but if you're not careful, you could miss them. Hearing you share your new relationship with the Lord lets me know that I can't be silent either.

"God was definitely working this morning. Right after that craziness with Vince, I, too, made a decision for the Lord! After you guys left the sanctuary and I got the minister to the bishop's office, I made a trip down the opposite hallway to the little chapel. If you haven't been there, it is something else. Well, it was there that I surrendered my heart to the Lord!"

"Sounds like that makes us brothers in Christ, C. J., if I recall what Mia used to say about Christian folks," Steve said, smiling. "But you know that little chapel you speak of in such a special way? Well, I guess I got there sometime after you did. And like you say, it is indeed a very special place to fellowship with the Lord; yes, it is."

"Yes, it is!" said C. J. "Yes it is! And isn't it fantastic that the door is still open, Steve! Man, oh, man! I'm overjoyed for you, Steve!

CHAPTER THIRTY-THREE

"MR. SHADOW, Mr. Shadow, wake up now. We be going to start breakfast very soon, and you need to be washed up so you can feed and all."

Shadow, squinting out of his left eye, saw a smiling, brown-skinned, middle-aged woman with small black eyes, looking down at him. When he opened both eyes to look up at his sleep intruder, he saw that she was dressed in a white blouse, a dark green skirt hanging well below her knees, and white stockings with brown, granny-like shoes. Her hair, with two or three ribbons running through it, was tied up in a bun.

He sat up from where he had been lying on the floor near the kitchen. In reaction to what the woman was saying, Shadow's immediate thought was, *I should tell this old woman to go away and mind her own business.*

But instead, he simply said, "Begging your pardon, ma'am, I didn't mean any harm. I was just waiting until you ladies opened up so I could catch a quick bite and be on my way."

"No harm done, son. I just kinda thought it mighty strange, you be sleeping out here when they be having beds and such in the Jensen Family Life Center. And what's this talk about 'being on your way'? Ain't you a part this here church? I knows you ain't a regular member, 'cause I knows every person who be a member; but since the strange happenings, all who have come since then are now considered members."

"Well," Shadow said softly, "that's a nice thought, ma'am, but I'm not planning to stay, so I won't be one of your 'members.' Now if I might be so bold as to get some of your tasty ham and cheese sandwiches and one of your cold drinks, then I'll be on my way. Thank you kindly, ma'am."

"Now Mr. Shadow, don't you be so fast to be leaving us. Where you gonna go? What you gonna do out there anyway? You don't know who out there and who is not . . . so you should wait and speak with our new pastor. He's a right nice young man, you'll see. I know he can help you with this here big decision that you want to make. I can go ahead and call him on that there intercom if you like. At the very least, you know, we be good Christian folk. So why leave?"

"Well, ma'am, that is real nice of you, for sure; but I'm really needing only the food I've told you about. Then I'll be on my way."

He thought, *Christians, these folks wouldn't know Christians from the man in the moon! Get saved! Become a Christian! Now why would I want to be tied down with all of them don'ts and dos anyway? That's all it is, you know; don't do this and do this instead! And I have yet to see any one of them here master this so-called Christianity stuff. Not a one of them has been nice to me; they all got that high and mighty holy attitude! You know, like they are better than anyone else! But there's nothing to be gained by debating this subject with this poor soul. What's the point? She's kind enough; no need to hurt her feelings. I'll just wait for the food and then I'm out of here! I just hope I don't run into any of these supposed Christians like that new young minister. He thinks he's hot stuff, I bet!*

AUTHOR'S NOTE

OVER THE PAST several years, I have grown to love the Old Testament. It is in those sixty-six books that one reads about man's blatant disobedience and disregard for the things of God. God, on the other hand, is revealed as showing much restraint with His love, mercy, and forgiveness. It is not too difficult to see that trend continuing even in these times. Interestingly, we have chosen to end this second novel on that dismal note—with Shadow in a disbelieving frame of mind and choosing to leave Saint Augustine.

For certain, we have left you, the reader, with many questions to ponder. What will become of Sister Minister now that she has had that piece of glass removed from her forehead? Will she become a human vegetable or a hardworking saint for the Lord? How will Steve and Joan behave now that they are new Christians? Have Randy and Sister Agnes actually witnessed a miracle? Has Carlos's seemingly thoughtless behavior served to weaken C. J.'s fragile faith?

Answers to these questions and others await you in the last and final novel of the trilogy: *We Have Not Been Listening: The Revelation*.

As this book comes to an end, I leave you with the following thought-provoking Scripture:

We Have Not Been Listening: The Awakening

For I do not want you to be ignorant of the fact, brothers, that our forefathers were under the cloud and they all passed through the sea. . . . Nevertheless, God was not pleased with most of them; their bodies were scattered over the desert. Now these things occurred as examples to keep us from setting our hearts on evil things as they did. Do not be idolaters, as some of them were; as it written: "The people sat down to eat and drink and got up to indulge in pagan revelry." We should not commit sexual immorality, as some of them did—and in one day twenty-three thousand of them died. . . . These things happened to them as examples and were written down as warnings for us, on whom the fulfillment of the ages has come. So, if you think you are standing firm, be careful that you don't fall! No temptation has seized you except what is common to man. And God is faithful; he will not let you be tempted beyond what you can bear. But when you are tempted, he will also provide a way out so that you can stand up under it.

(1 Corinthians 10:1, 5-8, 11-13 NIV)

CPSIA information can be obtained at www.ICGtesting.com
Printed in the USA
LVOW07s2238151015

458511LV00015B/224/P